The Dinner Party

Gordon Houghton was born in 1965 in Blackburn, Lancashire, and studied at Oxford University, where he gained a double First in English. He has been a pools collector, a wages clerk and the editor of a computer games magazine. *The Dinner Party* is his first novel.

THE DINNER PARTY

Gordon Houghton

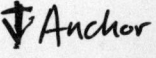

TRANSWORLD PUBLISHERS LTD
61-63 Uxbridge Road, London W5 5SA

TRANSWORLD PUBLISHERS (AUSTRALIA) PTY LTD
15–25 Helles Avenue, Moorebank, NSW 2170

TRANSWORLD PUBLISHERS (NZ) LTD
3 William Pickering Drive, Albany, Auckland

Published by Anchor – a division of Transworld Publishers Ltd

First published in Great Britain by Anchor, 1998

Copyright © 1998 by Gordon Houghton

A catalogue record for this book is available from the British Library

ISBN 1862 30034 8

Typeset in 11/14pt Adobe Caslon by Kestrel Data, Exeter

Printed and bound in Great Britain by
Mackays of Chatham plc, Chatham, Kent.

for M + D + J + J + J + R + ?
and, of course,
for K

THE DINNER PARTY

Let's be honest.

The only aspect of this whole business which in any way disturbs me is the thing in the sink. Everything else (the Rites, the Symbols, the Objects, the Collection – even the murder) has been the logical conclusion of my life so far: it defines me. But that thing, staring at me as if I were solely responsible, as if the whole universe hadn't conspired with me to produce these events, in this place, at this moment in time . . . that thing bothers me.

But I'm getting ahead of myself. As my father used to say: *If you want to tell a story properly, start at the start and end at the end.* Complete crap, of course – you can tell a story in any way you like – but I don't have much time, and I can't think of any better way to begin.

So:

I remember my own birth very clearly.

This might strike you as odd, unique even, and I understand that, I really do; but to me it's unexceptional. I've told my friends about it, and their reactions have warned me against broadcasting the information too widely. But – what the hell? – some stories just have to be told. Try to keep a thing down and it struggles and wriggles and wrestles until it slips from your grasp. My father, when I knew him, strangled many a motto, but there was one in particular which he squeezed so hard that he just about murdered the meaning, and it wasn't until long after he'd gone that it began to have any value for me. Even now, when I repeat it to myself, I can still hear his deep, slow voice: *Kill it or set it free*, he said, *but don't sit on it*.

I can't remember the exact circumstances in which he passed on this home-grown aphorism – there were too many to recount – but it's stuck to me like no other. I've got half-recollections of mundane, practical, less succinct proverbs dealing specifically with everything from never pouring hot fat down the sink to putting the washing powder back in the same place you found it, but this one has never faded. It's as much a part of my childhood as my pet rabbit, my favourite toys, and the open fire in our living room. It's reassuring, and timeless, like an old piece of furniture; but it must have started somewhere. My own special theory is that *the root of all life is sexual contact*, so I guess, in the end, like everything else, it was simply a result of personal erotic experience.

Don't sit on it, he said.

So I won't. I was there at my birth, and I remember. This is what happened.

*   *   *

It was very warm. About as warm as I am now, in fact (it was hot here when I first stepped in, but, unlike my mother's womb, this surrogate gets colder by the minute). It was also dark, and wet, and slightly sticky – though, of course, these evaluations only came later, when I realized that the world could be light, and dry, and smooth, and a thousand other distinct physical conditions. (Not to mention the huge scope of psychological states: since I popped out from between her thighs I've learned that you can be more than just annoyed or contented, that you can cry, and laugh, and use a sharp intake of breath to indicate that you're running out of patience, and . . . whatever.)

But let's go even further back. Most people remember little or nothing from before they were born. Even before they get to three, it's just simple sound-bites, a favourite toy, a nightmarish experience in hospital, a friendly face, sitting in the back of a car, their parents' legs. Memory can select any one moment from a million such random events and sensations – who knows why one is given preference over another? (Given time, I could probably even forget what happened today, and all I'd be left with is a vague sense of guilt, a hazy unease. But I don't *have* time.)

Anyway, in my case there's hardly anything I can't remember about my own life, no grey period in which the past was a mixture of the apocryphal, the half-remembered, the known. I *know* there was a time when I existed in two quite distinct worlds; and I knew that these worlds would be joined together, and that they would make a new world much stronger than either of its parents. Of course, when I talk about twin worlds you're probably thinking 'sperm and ovum'. But I don't think it's that simple. I've seen sperm under a microscope: nasty, single-minded, futile, repulsive, clueless, comical, rudderless, wriggling eels with outsize heads. And I know what a human egg looks like: mostly dull. But from what I can remember about myselves at that time, I was the perfect combination of awesome size and breath-taking beauty . . . Incidentally, I trace *all* my mood swings back to this original duality. Ever since I was born I've suffered violent fluctuations from misery to elation and back again – you try to maintain an even keel, but in the end it's easier to abandon ship.

I had no sense of time before the embryonic phase of my life, so I don't know *when* the twin worlds collided. However, their Joining was Significant. If I was writing this, I'd use capitals to distinguish between those events which have a bearing on the story you're about to hear, and those which have significance generally but don't mean much in this context. For example, this morning I tied my shoelaces in reverse order, left before right. This is insignificant, but is nonetheless one of many things that happened today. But the Joining *was* Significant because it was the first in a sequence of many rites of passage.

For all but the fortunate few such rites no longer exist. There is no threshold, no ritual to announce that beforehand you were one thing and now you have become another. For me, though, there have been many such sacraments. They all begin with fear and self-loathing, peak in ephemeral satisfaction, and decline to remorse.

This sequence has been the story of today, and is the story of my life.

In the womb I was conscious of just three facts.

The first – my divided history up to that point – I've just told you about, so I won't repeat it.

The second was my own existence, a state intimately connected to sound. I remember, in particular, two heartbeats. The background rumble of my own heart acted as a metronome, a clock regulating the cycles of activity outside my small, private sphere. But it wasn't always regular, and I attached great significance to minuscule fibrillations, out of all proportion to their importance. I've since copied this pattern of behaviour to excess, revering detail and rarely seeing the whole picture. And then there was my mother's heart. More distant, a sluggish pulse reverberating down the umbilical cord and throbbing at my belly. An accompaniment to my own music. I think of her, my mother, as a student imitating my lead, following almost perfectly, sometimes syncopated, but quick to pick the beat again.

There were other sounds, too, but these I classify as Discord: a dog barking, a car starting up, a plate smashing on the floor, the violent rushing of my mother retching into the toilet bowl. The biggest Discord of all was conversation, a hazy, meaningless mumbling which (at first) I believed was part of my own thoughts, my mind's attempts to sort the crap from the quality that would serve me in later life. It was a shock when I realized that these sounds were beyond my control. Anyway, there were two voices I distinctly remember which might have belonged to my parents, but – get this – *I can't be sure*. Don't dismiss this so easily: what concrete proof do any of us have that the people who claim to be our begetters actually did the begetting? I don't mean birth certificates, or old photos, or word of mouth, or the fact that you have his big nose and her thick lips – I mean real *proof*.

Take my case. My parents *never* spoke to me as a child in the same pedestrian and vapid tones they used when I was sprouting inside that swelling belly. This has often troubled me. It's a silly theory, and you won't entertain it for a moment I'm sure, but it has to be said (*Don't sit on it*): I believe that the two voices I heard in the womb did not belong to my parents. This leaves two conclusions. Either I was swapped at birth and everyone has kept very quiet about it since, or my parents hired surrogate speakers to talk to me *in utero*.

Consider my father's last words to me before he left: 'You're no son of mine. I never wanted you, and I won't have anything more to do with you.'

Before I reveal the third aspect of my life in the womb, I've got five scraps of information for you. Pay attention: all of these have some bearing on the events I'll soon describe.

1. These names are important: John, Alison, Nigel, Susan, Allan, Kate.
2. I have an *excellent* memory, so everything I've told you, and will tell you, is true.
3. Another name. My father's surname is Fly, so since I was a boy I've given him the nickname *Dragon*. Ha bloody *ha*. His family – I can't call them *mine* – emigrated to the West from eastern Europe, so it all fits in a spooky subliminal kind of way.
4. *My* name is Felix. Labels should be Significant, and the three events leading up to, and including, my birth made my label inevitable: I was born at seven o'clock on July the seventh; on the same day my father won a small bet he'd had with an uncle about the time of my arrival (he'd 'felt it in his bones'); and I took only ten minutes to slip out, from the bursting of the dam to the cutting of the cord. The fact that Felix is more suited to a cat, a Roman

dictator and a host of early Christian saints bothered no one.

5. I've never been a great communicator. It's not entirely my fault, and I can't say I regret it, but it's there. It can't be ignored. As a result, I've had a fear of conversation since childhood . . . But I do have friends, and I value them. The dinner party this evening is a case in point: I wasn't the most talkative member of the group, but I was happy with the way things went and satisfied that the appropriate rites had been properly carried out. More about that – and my friends – later.

OK. The third fact about my life in the womb:

I could see the future.

Think about that: *I knew what was going to happen.*

Everything was revealed to me by thought-pictures. Visions, if you prefer. These weren't destinations that could be altered, or prophecies about events affecting someone else if certain conditions were fulfilled, but things that would occur, without question, whatever I did. Sometimes they were simple images, such as knives, or spinning wheels, or blood; but most of the time they were hazy feelings. I was never given the complete picture – I would have thrown myself off a cliff at the first opportunity if I had – but there was always enough there for me to know that I would suffer accidents, and failure, and misery, and rejection. (This raised the question, which has been asked by millions before me, and will be asked by millions after I'm gone: *What, then, is the point of going on?* Like them, I don't have the answer.)

This foreknowledge wasn't too disconcerting at first: deep inside my mother's soft, protective shell I didn't know life could be anything other than the way I foresaw. I had no . . .

context. I didn't know much about beaches (except for that rhythmic hiss), or kites, or pets, or mirrors, or toys, or fire, or friends. The pictures I saw were cut-scenes, snatches of emotion – and the most prevalent emotion was fear.

The biggest and most frightening picture of all was also the clearest. It was like a story: you have an idea what's going to happen from the clues you pick up, but you never know exactly where it's going to end, or how all the details will slot into place.

The big picture was this. I knew that I was destined to harm, but until today I didn't know *who* would be harmed, or how it would be done.

2

But I haven't told you how I was born.

There was nothing to it. For my mother – well, it was all over so quickly she barely had time to work herself up into a scream. For me the experience was more shocking. I was too big to stay where I was, it's true, but birth seemed the least attractive alternative. Why couldn't the womb go on expanding to accommodate me? And why did this new world have to be so different from the old? No round softness, no food on tap, no darkness. All angles, all brightness. A chaos of geometry.

But she *wanted* me out. Make no mistake. She wanted me *out*.

* * *

This isn't one of those stories where the mother collapses and dies in clean soft focus, leaving the father to carry a dark but noble burden, which becomes a huge . . . a huge *albatross*, which he transfers onto the kid, and the kid grows up and gets bitter and tortures animals, and it's all explainable in some spooky kind of way. No no. No indeed. She did her duty. She shitted that melon, she pushed, and they pulled, and out, out, out I came. And I had a precious, fleeting moment of elation, because everything was as I had foreseen; and then a huge, invisible, doughy hand flew through the air and struck me squarely on the cheek. This was my first pain, and my first pleasure. It made me draw my first breath, and open my eyes. I've since had time to regret both, of course.

Is there anything more to be said? I'll skip the obscene sterility of that scene, that . . . *cage* of brightness, noise and people. I won't describe my mother's blood-stained thighs, the steely, sinister tools, the *hardness* of everything. I won't discuss the rough, dry faces, the old, wrinkled eyes, the immense, open mouths. But I *will* mention the worst thing of all (you've all been through it; it's no surprise):

One of those rough, dry faces took one of those steely, sinister tools and, in the blinking of a baby's eye, held it above my belly and sliced clean through the Cord. He cut the connection, like *that*, and nothing could repair it. And there were swabs, and dressing, and they held me to my mother's head, where I orbited for a while, like a small moon held in space by the doctor's arms, but nothing could . . . And I remember her jet black hair, hardly disturbed, a couple of tiny beads of sweat sliding down her forehead, and *nothing* could repair it. She seized me, kissed me, and when she pulled away, her lips were coated with a thin film of blood, and she drew me to her again, to her skin, and she held me there. She was salty, and warm, and I felt some new, some strange desire, some . . . hunger.

But nothing could repair me.

And who gives a fuck? Everyone goes through it.

Anyway, being born taught me one important lesson: *The world is a shuttle service from the slap to the kiss and back again.* It's melodramatic, it's not particularly succinct, but it's easily the most useful aphorism I've learned. It means that even when I don't know what will happen next, nothing can surprise me.

When I finish *this*, for example, I don't know what will happen next.

Will it be kiss? Will it be slap?

Will it be either?

I often reminisce about birth when I'm in the bath. (Did I tell you I was in the bath? I don't think so; it wasn't relevant until now.) Anyway, as soon as I dip my toes into the water, my mind ferrets for the memories. To enhance the experience I usually do it at night, sometimes with the lights out and the blinds drawn. It's a paradoxical ceremony. I feel safe, and comfortable; but at the same time I have an urge for self-destruction. *Suicidal* is too strong a word for this feeling, but in the back of my mind there is always the possibility that, this time, I won't be getting out. I began in the womb; I will end in its surrogate.

But I enjoy the nakedness and exposure, too. The rippling of the warm water over my skin. I can't cover myself all at once – the bath is slightly too small – so I alternate between submerging my knees or shoulders. This means I'm never satsified, so there's always something to do. Sometimes I try to remain still so that I can watch tiny specks of dust settling on the surface tension. Sometimes I create tidal waves with rhythmical body movements, stopping only when a bucketful of water cascades onto the red lino. Sometimes I turn on the hot tap with my left foot, as I'm doing now, to maintain a comfortable temperature. I never put oils or salts in the water, partly because they inflame fresh wounds, but mainly because it diminishes the purity of the ritual.

Tonight I'm . . . *content*. Physically, I mean. The dinner party was a success: everyone ate well, and the questioning was minimal. I'm usually a bit hungry even when I've eaten, but not now. I can't imagine eating anything ever again. Except for the chocolate Biscuits – which, as you'll soon see, are a necessity.

Let's face it. I'm avoiding the subject, aren't I? I'm *avoiding* it.

All this crap about birth and baths and the past, and all these dark hints, and I just can't get a grip on what I want to say about *now*, about *here*. All the stuff that happened today. And I want to explain it.

But it won't be forced. As my real father once said, *When the time is right, today will come*. It was a stupid comment, but I think I know what he meant.

Kate, and David, and the dinner party, and today – when the time is right, they'll come.

But before I do anything else, I need to set the scene. You're hearing this story from the most important room in the house, and you don't even know what the house looks like. Let me take you on a tour.

The bathroom, where I am now, is at the end of a wide hallway which runs virtually the entire length of the bungalow. This hallway contains a chest freezer – the upright variety is useless for large quantities of meat and vegetables; the baskets are always too flimsy, or too shallow – and along both the long walls there is a line of five shelves, which house a substantial part of my Collection. I'll tell you more about this later on. On the left-hand side there are doors leading to a storage cupboard-cum-cloakroom, and to the kitchen (which, in turn, has two more doors leading to the garden and to the integral garage, where I keep the rest of my Collection and the scalding tank). On the right-hand side another two doors take you into my bedroom (closest to the front door), and the living room, which faces south onto the back garden.

The freezer, now that I've mentioned it, used to belong to my parents. It still works well, but it's got a habit of defrosting spontaneously. All the food gets ruined, of course. When I was younger I used to be afraid of it, particularly when I was too small to see over the top. It was like a great white mouth, opening wide to disgorge the Sunday roast, then clamping shut again. Or it was like the monstrous white whale in *Moby Dick*, beached in our kitchen on the back of some freak tidal wave. My mother rarely left it open, but when she did, and when she left me alone, I would sometimes stretch on tiptoe to peer into its icy heart. (It scared me shitless, to tell the truth.)

It's not like the modern freezers either, which have doors you can open and close at will. If you fell in, it would take a few minutes before you could push open the door and climb out again. The thrill this gave me as a child – the thought that if I fell in, and if she had been distracted, I could have been trapped inside and slowly suffocated – well, it bordered on *ecstasy* . . . And as I grew taller I discovered that I could clamber up and sit on the edge, one side of me cold, the other warm, and live out the fantasy of danger.

I have a recurrent dream about freezers. Sometimes it's the one at work; sometimes it's the one in the hall. Always, the freezer is much deeper on the inside than it appears from the outside, and the lid (or the door) closes softly, almost without my noticing, and I'm plunged into darkness. I panic, and scrape my hands raw trying to find a way out, but (and this is the weird thing) after a while I accept what's happened, and hold my breath, and hold it, and begin to enjoy what's happening. Usually, it ends there, but last night it went on, and there was all sorts of other stuff, and – well, we'll get to it later.

The bathroom is small but always alive with light during the day. Come through the door and the bath itself lies along the right-hand wall, the sink is straight ahead, and the toilet is far left, in the corner. On the left wall there's a small shaving mirror and three shelves, and on the door behind is a hook to hang clothes. At the moment only my red dressing-gown hangs there, but earlier this evening when I was *obliged* to take another bath after preparing dinner, the peg was overburdened with underpants, trousers, and shirt. I can still visualize the early evening sunlight illuminating the bright colours, and the crazy patterns of the stains.

Against the wall, between the door and the bath, there's a table, on which I've carefully placed the Biscuits, a portable cassette recorder (the same one I'm using to dictate these memoirs), a towel, a cheap radio, and a telephone. The radio is one of the few comfortable reminders of my childhood. It's not that my family couldn't afford a television – we owned a black-and-white set for a few years, then rented a colour one when I was ten – but I grew to despise – despise *is* the right word – I *despised* the endless, numbing sequences of bland images. My head was bursting with pictures and arcane prophecies, and the radio complemented these with exotic words, which brought my imagination to life; but television was *interference*. (Except for the cartoons – and I only enjoyed them because the violence made me laugh out loud until I was nearly sick, and because I felt sympathy with the characters who lost control, who lashed out.) Anyway, the radio's been off since I got in. There's never anything interesting on after midnight.

I should tell you more about those shelves, because everything on them has some connection with the past. I'll start at the top.

I bought the six-pack of razor-blades to kill myself with in a particularly bleak, weak, self-indulgent moment, but ended up using them for wet shaving instead. The electric razor beside them has been redundant for years; I don't really know why I've kept it. It has never, in advertising-speak, shaved me close. But I can't discard anything I've used. You never know what its significance might be.

Next to the shaving tools is the shaving foam. This was bought exactly five years ago and hasn't been moved for the last four years, three hundred and sixty-four days. The side facing the light has faded to an uneven, pale blue. I've only used it once: I got a neck the colour of smoked salmon for three days. I've always had sensitive skin; I blame The Burning.

Next to the shaving stuff there's a bottle of aftershave, almost full. If the foam was like fire, the aftershave was like acid. I had to wear a cravat and an open-necked shirt for a week to disguise the rash. But, *darlings*, I was passing through a creative period at the time, so it wasn't *too* great a burden . . . Next to the aftershave is a styptic pencil. I daren't use this.

Along the rest of the top shelf there's a comb (covered in dandruff, bits of hair, and grease), a spare tube of toothpaste (half-empty), a plastic container of skin cream (colourless, odourless, flavourless), a cute nodding dog (which has lost its nod), and an empty can of deodorant.

Moving on down.

The middle shelf bears my girlfriend's marks – Kate's marks. Half a dozen cosmetic substances; a small tin, decorated with transfers of rabbits, full of tampons; a hair brush (clean); a yellow plastic duck; and a plastic container of skin cream (colourless, odourless, and flavourless again). Naturally, I can't look at these things without recalling her, without seeing her face, this afternoon.

Down again.

To the bottom shelf, and my five Objects, placed there just before I ran the bath tonight. They're arranged equidistantly, and I've drawn a protective circle of Symbols around each one. The Symbol system is my own. I don't feel I can tell you about the Objects yet, not until I've got a clear picture in my head of the routes by which they arrived here. The Symbols are straightforward, though. Put simply, they're naive representations of formative events, and have been part of my world-picture since childhood.

They are, in chronological order: a naked flame, a rabbit's foot, a bicycle, an erect penis and a razor-sharp blade.

Between the shelves and the toilet, there's a mirror. It's got a hairline crack running in an arc from the bottom left corner to halfway up the right side, which has been the subject of more jokes about ugliness and bad luck than . . . I don't know what. The fact that the glass has been broken for more than five years, and that the crack was caused by a half-hearted head-butt in one of my less controlled moments, interests no one.

Anyway, the point is this. The mirror terrifies me.

I've *never* trusted mirrors. I'm convinced that, when you're alone in the room with your back turned, they *watch* you. Like they've got someone trapped inside. Yeah, I know, it's funny. It's kooky. Prove it, prove it. Well, it *can't* be proved, of course – but *neither* can it be disproved. You can be sly and set up hidden cameras, as I once considered doing, and you can record what happens when you're going about your own business elsewhere, but the mirror is too smart. It's seen it all before. It *knows*.

And there's more. I believe that mirrors can act as portals to another world, that when the time and circumstances are right you can pass over the threshold and enter a new dimension . . . It happened to my father. Seriously. The last I saw of him, he was straightening his jacket, facing the mirror in the hallway. I was on the landing, and turned away briefly; but for just long enough. I didn't hear the front door close, I didn't see him leave, but when I turned back he was gone. The mirror must have sucked him in. It mesmerized him, it sang to him – whatever – but when he was close enough (I can see its surface liquefying, rippling, spreading outwards), it pulled at him, enveloped him, gently, inexorably. He couldn't scream because the liquid glass closed over his mouth, and he couldn't breathe because it sealed his nostrils. And it wouldn't have stopped there. It would have probed at his eyes, reached down his throat, pushed up his backside.

Well, it's *one* theory.

Small mirrors like the one in this bathroom are usually no

threat, though: the worst that could happen is that it might pull your hair through, or bruise your face a little. My advice, even so, is to do as I do: keep a pair of scissors or a knife nearby. Just in case.

One more thing. These aren't my only concerns about mirrors. I have other, more concrete reasons for disliking them, bound up with the Rite of Cutting and the Rite of Exposure. But again: when the time is right.

OK. The toilet and the bath.

The toilet bowl rises to the same height as the rim of the bath. Is that specific enough for you? Faint smells of vomit, blood and urine are emanating from it. Emanating. Good word.

I vomited after the dinner. It wasn't so much that the meal was rich, or that I was feeling particularly nauseous, but it seemed like the right thing to do in the circumstances. A fitting tribute to food of too high a quality to be merely digested, and a logical continuation of the ceremony which began, quite spontaneously, this morning.

The bath is a deep burgundy basin stretching along the whole of the wall. Behind my head there's a small shelf littered with shampoos and soaps. At my feet there's a narrow window and two chrome taps. I have to refill regularly; I try to keep a balance between the water draining through the overflow, and the level I prefer, just below the rim. And the temperature has to be right, too. Hot, but not so scalding that it takes your hairs off.

Now me. Picture this.

My body floats in the bath, like a slaughtered pig abused by a bored abattoir assistant. This description is neither ridiculous nor forced, but perfectly accurate. I'll tell you why (I'm proud of what I've achieved).

There are scars covering almost all of my body. These wounds are my history, a book of stories, some more interesting than others, all varying in length, shape and style, all unique. Some are deep and white and run from my neck down to my groin and beyond, carved in moments of great anguish and self-doubt, or during the closing moments of an important ceremony. Some are cut to create unusual shapes, such as the bicycle on my right calf just below the knee; or in Significant places, such as the flames that ripple along my left arm from the elbow to the shoulder, which come alive when my biceps are flexed. Most are small, seemingly inconsequential scratches, apparently without meaning; but these incisions are the essential background without which the great flourishes would have no context or merit. They are the result of year upon year of meticulous attention to the demands of the Rite of Cutting. Whenever I step into the bath and immerse myself in its uterine serenity, the agony of these scars reminds me of what I have done, what I have been.

Today, I showed Kate these long, soft ridges of self-mutilation for the first time.

Again, I'm leaping ahead. There are too many distractions, too many false trails leading away from the straight path . . . That *thing*. If someone were to come in now – well, the worst of it is that there would be no accurate record of the events. Questions would be asked, accusations made, and I would be convicted on the basis of a few trivial details. The whole picture will allow you to make a more considered judgement.

* * *

Finally, I should tell you about the sink. I must empty and clean it soon. The toothbrush holder, the two brushes and the toothpaste tube are all stained and need washing, too. I managed to hide it all – all this mess – from my friends, this evening. They were suspicious, of course. But when I told them that the toilet didn't work, which is true, and that the floor was flooded, they were reassured. I spread wet towels over it, so that if anyone had glanced through the frosted glass in the door the lie would be convincing. In the event no one bothered, though a couple did nip out into the back garden for a pee, and I got the impression that everyone left sooner than normal with a hint of embarrassed haste. Naturally, I'd already cleaned up the kitchen, the garage and the hallway, so there was no real problem. But the reality is, I just didn't have *time* to mop up all the blood in here, and most of what I did manage to wipe up has filled the sink to the brim.

So. No more rambling. You know where I came from. You know where I am.

When I think about what happened today, I know that this whole story began much earlier. There's a chain in time whose links we can't see until we learn how to stand back and study everything from a distance. I don't know if I'm using these links as a defence, or as a weapon. I tell myself that it was all an accident, a freak incident; but, equally, I understand that there was a beginning.

And the beginning was The Burning.

3

When she heard the screaming my mother threw down the receiver, and I could hear my father's voice, puzzled and distant on the other end of the line: 'Hello?' A pause. 'Hello? Are you there?'

She threw the blanket over the flames, grabbed hold of my playsuit, drew me up and set off for the bathroom, all in one movement. I watched my smouldering sleeves trail tentacles of smoke in her wake as she ran. My lungs were bursting with screams and choked sobs, but all the time, somewhere deep inside, behind the wall of pain, I was *happy*. Does that seem strange? I can only explain it in this way: I knew that nothing would ever surpass the intensity of this pain – the pictures told me that – but they also told me there would be times in the future when, if I followed the course laid down for me, I might have experiences of similar vehemence. As she plunged me beneath the running water in the bath, this prophecy was a powerful consolation. And that image is still so clear: the running water spiralling down the plug-hole, clockwise rivulets distorting the white ceramic, the cold tap shrieking with the pressure, her soft arms frantic with movement, and my clawed, shivering hands red and bloody from The Burning.

My parents' house was unremarkable. I remember mountains of brown tartan furniture, snow-capped with lace antimacassars, scorched yellow grasslands of carpet, a high sun glowing beneath the lampshade, and the pure white bathroom with its tiled cliff faces and its own freshwater lake. That bathroom is where the purifying ceremony of bathing began, as I sat naked with my mother, feeling the cold water soothe me, some animal part of me savouring the sensuous caress of her soft hands, secretly tasting her hot, salty tears as they fell on my face.

There are many factors I blame for the accident. If my father hadn't been working away, if he hadn't rung my mother at that moment, if the mechanical toy he sent me hadn't wound its way to the fire, if she had left the fire-guard in place . . . These are the major reasons; but there are many others, and chief among them is food.

She – my mother, that is – had just finished feeding me. After a long struggle I'd conceded defeat and sucked the bottle dry (I can still taste the milk, feel the teat on my lips). It was never very satisfying. When I grew older, I developed a taste for raw meat. Not chicken, obviously, but sometimes I managed to snaffle a slice of smoked bacon or a chunk of beef. The biggest treat of all was raw liver. I remember it lurking on the draining board like a huge, brown jellyfish, stranded at low tide. It wasn't until I left home that I realized there are some things which just aren't digested in polite company; experiences like this tend to remain private. And fantasies, too. I mean – for example – recently I've wondered how my diet would have coped with the placenta from my own birth. My mother could have kept it in the freezer, or in salt, until I was old enough to judge the taste for myself. The current fashion is to fry it in a little butter, perhaps with a few herbs and a dash of pepper, but I wouldn't have minded how it was prepared . . . It makes my mouth water even now. People don't understand desire.

Another example. I've occasionally discussed with my friends what they would do if, like those unfortunate people flying back to Argentina over the high Andes, their plane crashed and they were forced into cannibalism. Could they eat – and I mean sit down, chew and swallow – their fellow passengers, people with whom they'd survived the crash and struggled against death? As a child I had few problems with this idea. I even felt a mild wish to be trapped in the situation myself, just to show everyone that cannibalism is perfectly acceptable in the right circumstances, and that with a little preparation and disguise human flesh can even be palatable. Well, I'm not that child any more: the thought of eating people, even out of necessity, and however much it's disguised with sauces and skins, it just – it *repulses* me. I can accept others doing so if there's good reason (I would even carve the corpse if I thought it would help), but I'd rather starve than swallow the smallest sliver of human meat myself.

So anyway. She fed me, and normally we would have engaged in a few rites and observances of wailing and reward; but today was different. As soon as I'd finished, she pulled me out of the high chair, threw the bottle in the sink and carried me under-arm to the cot in the living room.

She didn't say a word.

This was unusual, and distressing. Generally, I liked the way my mother talked to me. She treated me more like a trainee adult than an eighteen-month-old child, and didn't expect me to say anything in return. Everyone else assumed that I only understood baby talk and that they needn't bother with real words because I was too stupid to know the differ-ence. (It happens everywhere, and it happens all the time. This is the way things are.)

With my mother, it was all a question of *tone*. She had a tone of voice which she only used when she was addressing me, and which I didn't appreciate until years later. It was detached from the rest of the infant world, with a slight vein of cynicism and humour. She would ask me questions while she was feeding me, or holding me, or kissing me: *Felix, what's it like being so short? Felix, most people think you're pretty, but you and me, we* know *that you're ugly.*

And so on.

Why was she so impatient?

She was expecting my father to call.

As soon as I was in the cot, the telephone rang (as it will ring here in ten minutes), and she used that tone again – *It looks like the old bugger just won't leave us alone* – before turning away and disappearing into the hallway. There was a brief pause before she picked up the receiver, then: 'Hello?' A loud, deep, faraway exclamation of pleasure came from the earpiece, and I knew it was my father. There was too much interference to hear exactly what he was saying, but I identified the rhythm of his words; then that, too, faded as my mother turned around, or held the phone closer to her head, or my father became less animated. But I continued to listen to one half of the conversation.

'He's fine. We're fine.'

I often picture my father standing in front of me, occupying the entire frame of my vision, thick and heavy like some distant cousin of the Neanderthals. I always suspected him of having some dark secret. He travelled around on business, though I've never discovered what his business was, or why you needed to travel to carry it out. Maybe this was his secret: he visited the continent every few months to call on his primitive cousins. I imagine him sitting around a fire, at night, in some middle-European cave, slapping everyone on the back and saying, 'Thag! Dag! It's me, Dragon! Nice to see you! Come and gnaw on this mammoth bone.' When I picture him, his face looms over me, like a student sculptor's first bust, riddled with deep, angular lines and thick folds, square-jawed and crude. People thought that with such a face he was violent and unfeeling. There *were* times when he meted out punishment, even a rare beating, but beneath it all there was – well, I don't know. He never showed me.

Another thing about my father: he was obsessed with money. He could talk for hours about cash flow, personal withdrawals, reconciliations and fixed assets; he could drone on and on about driving hard bargains, stitching people up, wheeler-dealing, and a thousand other business clichés. I suspect it was all a smoke screen. I have a vision that he was actually a well-spoken, nomadic accounts clerk, a mild-mannered and peaceful man who made steady progress and received moderate praise for his efforts.

'He's in his cot,' my mother told him.

(Pause.)

'Grumbling,' she added.

I hated that cot. It was built like a prison, despite all the transfers and toys and mobiles they decorated it with. I always associated it with punishment or indifference: they left me there when I whined, or when they grew tired of my meaningless conversations. Just discarded me. When my father was away the cot was always repositioned in the same place in the living room, where I could watch the sky through the window, or imagine that I was clambering up the slopes of the settee, or stare through the fire-guard into the bright yellow flames flickering in the fireplace. But today there was no fire-guard. She must have forgotten.

'Staring at the same four walls. He keeps me busy, at least.'

If I stretched I was just about tall enough to peer over the edge, but most of the time I had to sit and watch the world from behind bars. (Always so many bars. When I was fifteen, and in that dramatic way that teenagers have, I wrote a poem about the bars which have scarred my life, calling them *knife-cuts in the fabric of reality*. It embarrasses me to think about it now. My friend John, who's my partner in the butcher's shop where I work, is a better poet.) So I stretched, and I began to feel restless, thinking that if their conversation went on much longer I'd have to do something about it. I couldn't register a vocal protest, because I'd probably be blamed for everything that went wrong for the rest of the afternoon. She often became melancholic after she'd spoken to him, using up long silences listening to the radio or ironing. At least then I was let out of the cage; but if I tried to catch her attention too often it would exhaust her patience, and I'd find myself back inside.

'Nothing you'd call a *word*, exactly. More of a gargle.'

(I think they worried about my inability to speak. I didn't say a word until I was three, though I understood just about everything that was said well before then . . . What *was* the first word I uttered?

Shoe).

I grew much more restless. The fire was clamouring for my attention now. It distracted me from what *she* was saying, and my resentment of *him* for not being here to keep me occupied. I decided I wasn't going to be caged any longer. I had to escape.

'Hmm. This morning, in the post. He seems to like it.'

I knew what they were talking about, because I remembered the bright red parcel tied up with blue ribbon. She had unwrapped it for me after breakfast. Inside there had been a plain cardboard box (I still have it somewhere), rubber-stamped with these words, in blue ink: NOT SUITABLE FOR CHILDREN UNDER 2 YEARS OLD. I was allowed to open up the box, pull away the blue tissue paper and discover the contents for myself. The toy inside – a train – rapidly achieved Most Favourite Object status, and not just because my fish-like attention span usually translated *Most Favourite* as *Latest*. There was something magical about it, from its 2-8-2 black plastic wheels to its bright green smokestack. A pink plastic driver in a red boiler suit and cap waved from the footplate, his face locked in a grin. The rest of the engine was sky-blue, apart from the yellow key inserted into the panelling at the side. When you turned the key, the engine set off on a straight, determined course, making quiet *chuff-chuff* and *whirr* noises, winking happily with a flashing red bulb hidden beneath the chimney. Nothing could stop it. It glided over the thickest carpet, it bumped into furniture and turned around, and it took a thousand years to wind down. It was the perfect toy. And it lay there now, on its side, in front of me, beyond the bars.

I began to pull at the sides of the cot.

'Not so bad now. It was cloudy earlier on.'

The barrier slid upwards. She'd forgotten to lock it in place.

'No, I don't think so. It's supposed to be sunny.'

Squeezing through the tiny gap between the mattress and the base of the bars, I rolled out onto the floor with a bump, grabbed the train, righted it, and started to wind the key. It was a long, slow process, and I had difficulty turning it all the way, but eventually I pointed the smokebox door towards the settee, and let go. It *chugged* and *hummed* and banged into one of the legs, spun around and set off again. I followed it with my eyes, and watched as it ground to a halt against a pocket radio by the standard lamp. I stood up, walked over and freed it, treading on the radio, accidentally switching it on.

'I'm hoping he's gone to sleep.'

Quiet strains of a familiar tune came from the miniature speaker. I even recognized some of the words. *If you go down in the woods today you're sure of a big surprise*. This phrase has often worried me since. I could never decide whether the *surprise* was meant to be pleasant or nasty. And why would anyone want to go down to the woods anyway? Teddy bears having a picnic was not such a big deal. But it was their attitude to outsiders that bothered me, particularly when I heard the advice, *If you go down in the woods today you'd better go in disguise*. What kind of disguise did they mean? Dressing up as another bear? But that wouldn't fool anyone. Maybe you could uproot a tree, then – like Malcolm's men carrying Birnam wood to Dunsinane. A bit of fancy foliage and you were away, spying on their seedy little feast from a distance. But what really terrified me was this: what would happen if the disguise wasn't convincing enough? Did all those glassy black eyes and stuffed furry bodies suddenly turn towards you, pull out hidden hooks and hack you to death? This bothered me as a child. I recalled all my crimes against bears – a catalogue of severed heads, arms ripped out at the sockets, slashed stomachs, eyes gouged out – and wondered if their legal system operated on an eye for an eye basis . . .

Anyway, when the song stopped so did my dreaming. I found myself two feet away from the fire, and very hot. I didn't pull back, though: the train was scrambling to get over the edge of the decorative stone slabs in front of the fireplace, and I gave it a gentle push to help it on its way. It clattered along until it reached the grating, where it stopped again.

Come and help me, it said. *Help me into the fire.*

'I think I left the radio on.'

I looked into the fire. *Help me in. The fire can't harm you.*

Another tune, one I had never heard before, began on the radio, and I watched the flames dancing in time to the music. Left and *right* and left and *stop*. They amused me. I put out my hand towards them, and immediately pulled back in pain. *You said they couldn't harm me*, I thought to the train. And the train replied persuasively, *They can't. You only think they can. But look deeper, and forget about what you feel. Look deeper, and see what you can see.* So I looked harder, and I saw that there was something behind the brightness and the dancing and the terrible heat, something shadowy and vigorous. I squinted but couldn't get a clear hold on what it was. Almost imperceptibly I felt older, and my head flooded with visions of rabbits and bicycles and mirrors. And I laughed. They were silly pictures, but I liked them, and wanted more. *Get closer, then. Look behind the fire.*

The flames changed. Where there had been leaping tongues of light licking at the darkness, spitting crackling fragments of coal, now there were only animated pencil sketches. Harmless.

Harmless and cold. There were hundreds of them, piling high above each other, shimmering in and out of focus. *It's cold. Put your hands in. Push them aside. See what you can see.*

'I should turn it off. It might wake him.'

I reached in, and at first there was a strong stinging sensation which shot up my arms and racked my whole body; but it disappeared almost immediately. The flames *were* cold, after all. The pencil drawings fell away from my outstretched hands, and fluttered into the air like small, white butterflies, their absence revealing the rabbit I'd seen. That, too, disintegrated, leaving behind a spinning bicycle wheel; and when that fragmented and fluttered away, I saw my father standing in front of a long, thin mirror. But there was one final image, further in, deep inside the fire, much clearer than all the others. It showed two silhouettes; a man and a woman. They were moving against each other. At first I thought they were dancing, like the flames, but then I saw that she was cowering, and that he was holding something in his right hand. He raised it as the woman raised her arms; then he swung it down onto her, and she crumpled beneath him. Black fluid sprang from her neck, but he didn't stop. He did it again, and again, and again, and he didn't stop.

I began to scream. I heard my mother throw down the receiver and rush into the living room. Her face lost all colour when she saw my raw, red hands and the burning playsuit. She grabbed a blanket from the cot and smothered my scorched flesh with it, then bundled me up and carried me to the bathroom. As we passed the phone in the hall I could hear my father's voice, puzzled, distant, loud on the other end of the line:

'Hello . . . ? Hello? Are you there?'

4

That's the telephone – *just* as I predicted, may I remind you. How can we do this . . . ? I'll turn up the recording volume and put the receiver by the microphone, so you can hear what's being said.

'Hello, this is Felix. I'm sorry, but I can't come—'

'Felix? It's me, John. Stop pretending to be your answering machine.'

'It's one o'clock in the morning.'

'I know, I know, and I'm sorry for ringing so late. I woke up about half an hour ago, and I just couldn't settle again. I reckoned you'd be asleep, and I thought I'd leave a message. I did say I'd call—'

'You did indeed.'

'—and I have. I'm sorry if I woke you.'

'You didn't. I've been awake since you left.'

'Oh. Something up?'

'No. I just – I don't know. I need to get away. From here, I mean. Go away and think. It's all I've been doing since you left.'

'Right . . . And?'

'Well. Nothing, really . . .'

'Yeah, *yeah*. What is it?'

'OK. I'll tell you. But don't laugh.'

''Course I won't.'

'Well don't, even if you want to. It's serious, for once. Um . . . I've been making a tape. A recording of what I've been thinking. I've been lying here for the last hour or so sorting things out in my head. Framing them. Trying to get things straight. I've gone through all the things I've done in the past—'

'Uh-huh.'

'—I've gone through all those things, and I've looked for a pattern, and there *is* a pattern. I've been trying to escape from it, but it's all there. It's always been there. You can't escape.'

'Uh-*huh*.'

'You said you wouldn't laugh—'

'And I'm not. It's just that you're not making much sense. Anyway, why now? Why do you have to go over everything tonight?'

'I just *have* to.'

'Is it Kate? Has she got something to do with all this?'

'Sort of. She's the thing that sparked it off, but there are other things, too. I'm not right. In my head it's all right, because I've got reasons, but if you stand back and look at things, at what I've done, and who I am, none of it's right . . . Look, I'm sorry for being so vague, but I can't tell you what it's all about just yet.'

'Sounds serious.'

'I don't know whether it is or not. That's what worries me. I just haven't got any reference points to compare it to . . . Are you there?'

'Yeah. I was just thinking. Can I come and see you tomorrow?'

'No. I don't know. My father's coming, and I'm not sure I want to be around when he does. The thing is, I had this idea – an idea of leaving him the tape. There's going to be loads of stuff about him on it. And I'd rather you weren't mixed up in it all.'

'Where are you going?'

'Somewhere you don't want to come.'

'Well—'

'Look, I'm sorry. Forget everything I've said.'

'Um—'

'And I'll see you on Monday.'

'OK. Are you sure you're—'

'Yeah. I'm as happy as a clam that's just been voted Clam of the Year by its fellow bivalves.'

'Hmm. Well, look after yourself.'

That was John. He's my business partner, if you recall. And since he's just rung me, this is as good a time as any to start telling you about my friends. I don't know how I'll do this. Bit by bit, maybe. Whatever: you need to know something before I start talking about the dinner party; it's no good me suddenly saying, *Nigel said this*, or *Alison said that*, if you don't know anything about them. Alison, for example—

Hang on. Why was he ringing me?

*   *   *

'Hello?'

'John? It's me, Felix.'

'Felix. I was just trying to get back to sleep.'

'Uh-huh. Tell me something first.'

'What?'

'Why did you ring me?'

'Um . . . I just wanted to see how you were. And to talk. If you can't sleep yourself you might as well try to wake someone else up . . . Look, the reason I keep asking if you're all right—'

'Yeah?'

'—it's because you didn't look too comfortable at dinner. You kept squirming about. Like you had a hair shirt on.'

'I was tired.'

'Yeah, *sure*.'

'No, really. It's been a long day.'

'At least you didn't have to work. I spent *hours* doing the pigs' feet.'

'What was our apprentice up to?'

'Picking his nose and frightening kids. And making the scratchings, when he felt like it. I keep hoping one day he'll lock himself in the cold store.'

'Yeah. We could wait till the next morning and hang him up in the back of the van—'

'And drive him to the abattoir, and drop him in the scalding tank, without really looking. A terrible accident.'

'A tragedy.'

'We'd just have to grit our teeth and get over it somehow.'

'Why go to the abattoir for a scalding tank? We could always use mine.'

'Don't tempt me. It'd be too easy.'

'He's too tough, though. And too skinny. He wouldn't turn in a profit . . . By the way, what did you think of dinner?'

'Oh, well, my contribution was easily the most popular dish. The rest of the meal was OK, but a bit of a disappointment, I'd say.'

'Uh-*huh*. What d'you think the others thought?'

'Felix, apart from you, I think everyone had a great time. And before you say it, it *wasn't* the Free Feed Factor. If I was to select one thing, I'd pick those five sausages. I must have the recipe. And I don't want any of that rabbit meat crap. You might've been able to fool everyone else with that story, but not me. So what was it?'

'Wait until Monday.'

'Ooh. Aren't *we* an enigma?'

'We are.'

'Have you fixed the toilet yet?'

'Um . . . no. Did you mind?'

'Nah. Alison and I went outside anyway. I saw a few crossed legs by the end, though. What happened . . . ?'

'Just an accident. I made it sound a bit more dramatic than it actually was.'

'. . . only I sneaked a look through the glass when you were getting dessert, and there were towels all over the floor.'

'It's all sorted now.'

'Good, good . . . Well, look. We've run out of things to say, and I'm off to bed anyway, so I'll let you get on.'

'Yeah. Right. Well, good night then.'

'Good night, Felix.'

I considered telling him about what had happened. Really I did. I could have just said it, as a bare fact, and that would have been it. He would probably have taken it as a joke at first; but then I would've had to go through all the hassle of saying *I'm putting down the phone now, John. I can't tell you any more. I just can't, I'm sorry*. In the end it's easier to keep quiet. I could even have told him the truth about why I was squirming during dinner:

Anyone would squirm with these wounds.

Where was I?

Friends. I was going to introduce you to my friends.

I have five in all – excluding Kate, my girlfriend – and all of them came to the dinner party tonight. Otherwise I wouldn't be telling you about them, would I? No indeed. Curiously, I've never had *more* than five friends. I can't explain it. Anyway, our little group has not always comprised the same people. John, for example, only entered the scene about four years ago, though he's now the closest. Alison appeared two years ago. And so on.

Well, I could go on, but I won't. Before I get down to individuals, here are five general points.

1. All my friends have black hair.
2. None are couples. However, they have, in effect (though not in practice), all slept with each other – if you'll forgive the euphemism. I say *in effect*, because there was no orgy during which everyone made sure they were penetrated by everyone else; but they *are* all linked. X has slept with Y, who has slept with Z, and Z has slept with A and B. So X is linked to B, if you see what I mean. Anyway, their sexual encounters are a constant surprise to me. An intricate network of revelations, which I've never been part of. (I was a virgin until last night, so you can forgive me my naiveté, if nothing else.)
3. They've all had cycling accidents. It's a bizarre way to choose your friends, I know, but even if you don't

understand yet, I hope you will soon – bicycles have great Significance for me. Anyway, as a result, I've given each of them a secret nickname connected to the type of accident they suffered. These might appear ridiculous (I thought so myself at first) but, like any name, you get used to them. In no particular order, they are: Saddle, Handlebars, Cone, Wheel and Ditch. I've only told John his accident nickname, and he doesn't mind. The rest live in ignorance. That's what friends are for.

4. This is how long I've known each of them: one, two, three, four and five years. Blessed be the numerical sequence.

5. They're all omnivores. Allan is the closest to being a vegetarian, but he used to work in a sausage factory, so it's understandable.

Why am I describing them here, when you haven't even met most of them yet? For this reason:

The story of the dinner party is wholly self-contained. I don't want to mess it up by introducing new characters, telling you all about them, and breaking up the narrative. It would *spoil* things. So I'll introduce each of my friends at appropriate moments.

Starting with John.

5

John, John, friend number one. What more can I say?

Quite a lot, as a matter of fact.

He's my partner in the butcher's shop. I've known him for four years. He's older than me. We were apprentices together, working for the Unspeakable Butcher, Whose Acts of Cruelty Shall Never Be Described. Shortly afterwards he inherited a hundred thousand pounds from a rich uncle, who was 'something in shipping', or wine, or whatever it was; John's never said exactly what. (We both have our secrets.) I asked him once why he hadn't done something more with his money. He said that although one hundred thousand pounds sounded like a lot, it wasn't enough for him to live off for the rest of his life, and it was too little to spend on trivial gifts. So he invested most of it in the business and the equipment, and gave the rest away. Oh – and he walks with a limp. This is why.

His father bought him a bike when he was quite young. About six, I think he said. He'd graduated from scooters to tricycles to two-wheelers with stabilizers, and the day the stabilizers came off was when the accident happened. (I have *never* in my entire life fallen off a bicycle, though almost everyone I have ever known has. My father did. My mother fell off without moving. Darren, our apprentice, has fallen off his motorcycle, but won't say whether or not he ever owned a bike, or if he did, whether he ever fell off it. And David, of course . . . Well, I'll discuss him later. I can't face him yet.) Anyway, John celebrated his freedom by riding up to an old quarry just outside the town where he used to live, and he started practising a few stunts – easy ones at first, then increasingly risky. He didn't know it, but after his father had bought the bike he'd altered the height of the saddle; but he hadn't tightened any of the bolts properly, and all that juddering about in the quarry loosened the seat, and the saddle fell off just as John launched himself high into the air from an earth ramp. For a while he flew in blissful ignorance – until he hit terra firma, when the tubular metal seat support rammed into his right buttock. (Are all of us predestined to ride flying bicycles, waiting for that painful landing?) Anyway, John has since said that his experience *caused the kind of pain that can only be known, never described*. I asked him if it was like being buggered, but he only looked at me strangely. And that, ignoring the visit to the hospital, the X-rays and one severely damaged coccyx, is his story.

6

More friends later. In the meantime, I want to return to that image of the rabbit I saw in the fire. Why? Because it explains one of my personal Symbols, it's where the Rite of Cutting began, it reveals something about Kate, and—

Well, why don't I just get on with it?

To begin with, you should know that I'm engaged in a constant dialogue with my childhood. Some people prefer to bury the past, treating it as if it were some old relative who stayed with them for years, lapsed into embarrassing habits, and finally, thankfully, keeled over. Others hide their history down a deep well, pulling it up only when necessary to check that it's still alive. A few embrace it, make it comfortable, and ply it with treats until it starts to gossip.

I'm one of the few. I talk to my childhood. I ask it questions, and (when it can be bothered) it digs up memories, adding new links to the chain connecting past and present. It's not always a reliable source: its revelations are a combination of the truth, the half-truth and everything but the truth. I have to judge for myself which are the blind alleys, and which the paths of righteous confession.

Anyway, this is how it works.

It begins with a packet of Biscuits. Chocolate sweetmeal. The brand doesn't matter. The point is: Biscuits were my staple nourishment as a child, and are essential elements in persuading the past to speak up. It doesn't always work, and I don't always do it, but I'll try now. Just this once. Just for you.

After all, there's no truth without embarrassment.

So. I eat a Biscuit (as I'm doing right now) and I consult the child within. He's just one of my homely inner voices; for the sake of argument, let's call him *Child Fly*. I tell him I've been wondering about the rabbit. I've mentioned it a few times in this narrative already, and I can't quite recall the *exact* circumstances which led to its foot becoming one of my five key Symbols.

And Child Fly, a little critical, a little tetchy because he doesn't like being disturbed, replies with, *Your memory is so pathetic—*

And I have to interrupt him, of course. I have to be *firm*. I tell him I don't need the lecture. I just need the story.

This calms him down. *All right*, he says, *I'll tell you. It all began with the cracks in the pavement.*

My thought-pictures disturbed me. As soon as I began to recognize – I mean *really* recognize – the misery they predicted, I was frightened. But the images were often more than a little cryptic. (For example: I'd known as a baby that I was going to disfigure my hands in some accident involving fire, but the pictures revealed nothing about the telephone, or the train, or the radio.) So, when I was eight years old, I decided I needed some assistance, something that would help clarify their Significance; and I became interested in the instruments and methods of divination. That sounds very *grand*, doesn't it? But it was innocent enough to begin with: I reasoned that, since each thought-picture could be interpreted in a variety of ways, I should set myself tests which would help me select one interpretation above all the others.

For the very first test I needed just two tools: a piece of chalk and a pogo stick. With the chalk I marked out a rectangular course on the pavement outside our house; with the pogo stick I intended to negotiate the course. (It was important that there were a number of cracked paving slabs around too, for reasons you'll discover in a moment.)

It worked like this. One of my thought-pictures showed my father straightening his jacket in front of a mirror, in a house I didn't recognize. He disappeared briefly, then reappeared, dressed differently. And that was *all* I saw (not much help, I think you'll agree). Anyway, I considered two meanings: a) that in the future my father would examine himself in this mirror on two different occasions; or b) that a man who looked like my father would attempt to usurp his position in our family. To discover the truth, I jumped on my pogo stick and hopped once around the course: if I landed on a crack, it would mean that an impostor would attempt to replace my father; if not . . . Well, I've never had a good sense of balance, even before the Cutting began, and, of course, I landed on a crack. Option b) took root in my mind.

Some visions were even more vague – so vague that they

called for refinements in the ceremony. So, when there were more than two interpretations, the course length increased and the choice rested on *how many* cracks I collided with. If there was a borderline decision, I had to make two runs to clarify the situation. And if there was one interpretation which was far more plausible than another, I had to alter the rules yet again.

I'd like to say it worked, and I was happy with it, but Child Fly is telling me different. He points out that it was reliable for fifty-fifty decisions, but for anything else it was useless. In particular, he reminds me of the single incident which *convinced* me it wasn't a valid method:

The end of the world.

I had this vivid waking dream in which a huge building framed by darkness was on fire. Its windows shook, and shattered, and dripped with water; and people were screaming and throwing themselves to the ground, and . . . well, the dream ended there. But it terrified me. It could only mean one of two things: either the end of the world was nigh, or my thought-pictures were deceiving me. I was afraid to uncover the truth. I was physically sick. I delayed the ritual for a couple of days, and then (reluctantly) climbed on my pogo stick and sprang into action. The result confirmed my worst fears: I landed on a crack again. The world would be destroyed in my own lifetime! For weeks afterwards I wondered whether I should tell anyone, but eventually decided that doing so would cause mass panic. Everyone was better off in ignorance.

About a year later I sneaked into our local cinema to watch a re-run of *The Towering Inferno*. The waking dream came to life on the screen: the burning building, the fake screams, the water from the burst tanks spilling through the shattered windows. It was an awful shock. One disaster movie had undermined my whole system of belief.

Child Fly tells me I'm overstating the case. *At the time you just thought a better method was called for*, he says. *You were getting bored with bouncing over paving slabs anyway, and the neighbours kept complaining about the state of the pavements. Besides, you got caught nicking the chalk from school.* I doubt that it was really so simple – but he's persistent. *Listen to me. Forget about the big Significance for a moment. Everything is linked. Everything has equal value. The more questions you ask the more you learn. Give me another Biscuit, and I'll tell you what happened next.*

I know what he's talking about. The Sacrifice.

But he surprises me.

Not yet. You still needed a cipher for the thought-pictures. There were new methods, new observances. And after you'd tried and failed, there was the girl on the beach.

For two years after the failure of the pavement prophecies I experimented with established rituals. The classic ones that everyone knows about. I borrowed a book from the library and studied everything from alectryomancy to the zodiac. But the ceremonies were difficult to stage, and nothing really helped.

Take the first one: alectryomancy. I was too young to get hold of a real cockerel, so I used one of my old toys: a clock-work chicken which walked, pecked and clucked when you turned the key. But the ritual was still a total disaster. In a clearing in the wheat field behind our house, I drew a circle of the letters of the alphabet. I began placing sunflower seeds on each letter (it should have been corn, but that was too difficult to come by). I prepared myself mentally . . . But the chicken pecked at the wrong time, or wandered around in circles, or simply toppled over. Then my mother shouted for me, and when I finally got back I forgot where I'd left the toy and spent half an hour trying to find it again.

But, at last, I managed to make something happen. I placed three seeds on each letter as the ritual demanded, drove a stake into the earth, tied the clockwork chicken to it, and watched. It worked well enough: the bird wandered off in random directions, reached the end of the string, and eventually pecked at one seed or another. It was only when I was halfway through this ceremony that I realized I'd forgotten to ask any questions which it could answer. For some weeks I'd been shown a recurrent image which I just didn't understand. My hands and arms were covered in blood and thick black hairs, and my skin was shivering – and I couldn't make sense of it. I needed precise words or significant combinations of letters to clarify things, and I'd read that alectryomancy would help. So I sat down next to the circle, cross-legged, with my arms folded, and asked the question, slowly and clearly:

'What does this vision mean?'

The bird whirred and pecked a seed lying on the letter X, before falling over (would I trap my arms in a xylophone?). I moved it back to the centre, wound the key once more, and watched as it wandered over to the P (perhaps I was to die in an eXPlosion?). But it didn't stop there. It swerved to the left and headed back to the X instead, where it pecked at the same seed. I grew very angry.

'*Double X?*' I shouted. 'What does *double X* mean?'

In disgust, I ran home and left the toy where it was, tied to the stake. I expect it's there still, a heap of faded, rusted metal in a big, yellow field of wheat.

I tried many other methods, each with its own story, but generally there was always some drawback, usually a material difficulty. For example, I couldn't try axinomancy because I couldn't find a piece of jet. I had no arrows for belomancy, no shoulder-blades for empyromancy, no liver for hepatoscopy, and no crystal globe, or precious stones, or polished quartz for crystallomancy. I couldn't face raising the dead for necromancy, even if I'd known how to; and casting lots simply didn't make sense. Just about every method failed. During botanomancy, a sudden gust of wind blew away all the leaves of paper on which I'd written possible interpretations of a persistent dream. I had some fun with phrenology, but all I learned from the bumps on my head was that I was a stable, sensible person who would be kind to animals. Tasseography provided some vague images of rabbits and knives for a while, but at about that time my family switched to tea bags, and I couldn't pursue the interest any further.

I did have *some* limited success. I tried bibliomancy and landed my finger on the confusing biblical passage, 'he who fails to reach a hundred will be considered accursed'. But since I wanted to know the meaning of a thought-picture which showed me standing naked before a mirror, this didn't help.

In the end, chiromancy was the only ritual which worked. And only when I combined it with the Rite of Cutting.

Child Fly insists that I've provided enough examples. I can hear him giving me this advice: *Don't get drowned in detail. If you can't control yourself, I'll have to ration your memories.*

But I haven't finished this part of the story yet. I need to add that I realized long before I made the Sacrifice that none of these traditional methods could really work, and that I would have to create my own *personal* rituals again.

If I was going to use any object to unlock the meaning of the thought-pictures, it had to be something close to me which could generate random results. So I borrowed a die from an old Cluedo set and used it in a similar way to the pogo stick and pavement method. It worked for as long as I had simple choices to make and was sure enough of the correct interpretation to weigh the odds in my favour. But in the end I realized I was just living the future on the throws of a die – an aleatoric existence.

Child Fly hates it when I chuck the big words around. He's threatening not to tell me *why* I gave up using the die and hit upon the idea of the Sacrifice. I call his bluff. I tell him that even though I can't remember the *whole* story, I can remember *plenty* without his help.

But he sees through me straightaway.

If you recall, he says, *it was all because of the sand-castle, the sea-water and the girl on the beach.*

He's right, of course. But I sometimes wonder if he needs a little correction. His petulance can be very irritating.

Spare the rod, and so on.

Whatever: we're getting closer.

I'm on holiday, at the seaside. All my childhood summers melt into one high sun in a cloudless blue sky. There is the golden beach, and the shingle where I sink to my knees and run my hands through the pebbles. Further along the coast are red rocks, and small cliffs, and caves, and hollows. I plunge my arms into the tidal pools and uncover crabs. When I'm tired, I return to the sand, take my spade and dig, half-observed by my parents. I have been alive for ten years, and nothing is as beautiful as now.

I build a castle by the water's edge, piling sand from the moat onto the sloping battlements. I pack defence upon defence, an outer parapet guarding an inner curtain wall, with a great hall, a high watch-tower and a chapel for the knights, so that they can live, fight, and pray in my honour. I excavate a deep, narrow channel from the moat to the sea, and the tide rushes in, one great wave filling the ditch in a single movement, then draining away; filling and draining again with each successive wave. I line the moat with seaweed and packed sand, and pierce a frond of weed with a piece of driftwood, raising it on the tower as a banner. The moat fills again, and stays full, swirling with sandy, dirty sea-water.

The sun is sinking. I see a girl running in my direction, laughing. She's slim and pretty, with black hair shining in the sunlight. My age. She's wearing a vivid red and yellow swimming costume, and as she moves, the patterns shimmer in the heat, and she is on fire, a running, twirling flame leaping and dancing over the beach towards me.

In the moat the grains of sand settle; the water clears briefly. There's a temporary reflection of the girl, rippling and fragmented. But it's not a perfect likeness. It's much older than the ball of fire rolling along the shore. A taller, uglier vision, completely naked, with breasts, pubic hair, and long, thin legs. She's standing in a dark world surrounded by red shapes, some still, some swinging. There are silver lights flashing in the water, but it's gloomy, and I can barely see the shadow approaching her. It lowers her to the floor, gently, without a hint of violence; climbs on top of her; begins to rise and fall, with increasing vigour. The shadow and the girl turn over, and over again, and again more quickly, and fall into a spin, until nothing remains but a whirling blur. The water ripples, the sand stirs, the vision disappears.

But there's something else disturbing the surface. I reach down into the moat, far below where the sandy bottom should be, down almost to my shoulder, and I find something. Soft, solid, slippery, heavy. I pull it free from the sucking sand and it floats gently upwards to the surface. But the blood comes first, a dark red stain mingling with the sand and water, spreading to the castle walls. Half a second later a body bobs to the surface, sinks again, then settles half-submerged.

It's a dead rabbit.

I am screaming. The girl on the beach is gone. My mother is running to catch me in her arms.

Was it real or just a hallucination? Child Fly is convinced:

It vanished, didn't it? What more evidence do you need? Personally, I blame the ice-cream van. They must have been spiking the 99s.

At this point I have to tell you that I don't just speak to my *childhood* — I also have the occasional conversation with my teenage years. For the sake of consistency, I'll call this part of my past Teen Fly. Teen Fly is contrary, has no social graces, and lacks all semblance of charm; but if I want to make sense of what happened back then, I have to indulge him.

Why am I mentioning this?

Because Teen Fly claims to have something more to tell me about the girl on the beach. I tell him that there *is* nothing else. The story ended with the Sacrifice down by the canal, when I returned from the holiday. The vision was a clear message. I followed the instructions, and that was it. Finished.

Wrong, Teen Fly says. *The vision was over, but it wasn't the last time you saw her.*

I realize this. The Sacrifice told me she'd eventually become my girlfriend.

But, he insists, *I'm talking about between then and now. You met her again, just once — and I think you'll recognize that it was a warning, one you should have paid attention to long before today.*

I don't remember this.

Of course not, he adds smugly. *That's why I'm here.*

I'm at a school disco, my eyes closed tight, shutting out everything but the music. I've long since stopped trying to dance, compromising with a half-shake, half-bounce movement which looks odd but attracts attention. Attention is important. It concentrates my mind on other people. If I allow the thoughts to turn inwards they scavenge for darkness and bring it to the surface.

Child Fly wants to say something to Teen Fly here. I can't stop him.

Cut the melodrama, will you? If there's one thing I can't stand it's this bloody teenage Angst. Where are the beaches? Where's the laughter? It's all miserable dances, and self-denial, and stabbing yourself to death.

The *pair* of them.

The music stops, I open my eyes. I feel empty, and wander over to the bar for a refill.

'A mineral water, please.' I'm hungry. 'And a packet of peanuts.'

'Have you got a light?'

I turn around, and she's standing there. Her hair is still black, still shining. Her face is virtually the same as the one that repulsed me in the vision, a little younger maybe, but now I find it pretty.

She holds out an unlit cigarette. I notice a row of thin, white scars on her left wrist, like a tiger's stripes.

'I don't smoke.'

'Then I suppose I'll have to use this.'

She pulls a Lighter from the pocket of her black jeans, turns the wheel with her thumb, and sets the world on fire. I step back from the flame into a bar stool, though I'm spared the humiliation of falling. She laughs.

'Sorry. It was just a joke.'

I gaze at the huge, yellow, flickering light framed by a thin line of darkness. I can hear it rumbling, quietly, above the background conversation; I can feel its distant heat. My hands begin to itch and the fine scars on my face tickle for a moment, until she extinguishes the flame.

'It's all right,' I tell her. 'It's not your fault . . . What's your name?'

'Kate,' she says.

That's the end of Teen Fly's contribution, for what it was worth. I'll have to call him back in a while, of course – but I'll spare you his idle chat when I do. He'll help me understand what happened to David, and where the bicycle scar fits in.

(If you don't mind, I'll pause briefly here. The water's rippling against the slope of my belly, and it's cold. I'm shifting position to submerge it, raising my knees instead.)

OK. I want to finish this thing off. I want to head straight for the Sacrifice. I want to know how the rabbit died.

Child Fly wants more Biscuits.

It's a day or two after the holiday, and I'm finally unpacking, shaking out the sand from shoes and socks, throwing the dirty washing into the corner of my bedroom, tossing my new toys into the cupboard, and so on. I'm impatient, because the vision in the moat was a sign. The sign said: *You have been obsessed with irrelevant rituals. You have the power to understand your own future. But understanding requires sacrifice. And sacrifice requires a victim.*

I take my pen-knife and place it carefully, and with a sense of ceremony, into my jeans pocket. I leap down the stairs, brush past my mother, rush into the garden, open the door of the hutch, drag out the rabbit. It tries to pull back, but I grasp it by the ears and tug hard. Its claws scrape on the wooden floor through the sawdust, its hind legs rattle against the wire mesh, bang against the feed bottle, swing through the air into my midriff. It's a large rabbit, and I struggle to carry it all the way to the canal. The distance is no more than a mile, and for the most of the way it rests in my arms like a baby, rarely moving. But it's heavy and awkward, and when its weight shifts its claws dig into my skin, drawing blood. I walk most of the way, but as I reach the brow of the final hill I can't resist a sprint, still clutching the victim to my belly . . . And I'm too keen, too frantic. I stumble down the far side, and tumble over and over until the level ground slows my descent by the tow-path.

The rabbit lies on the grass beside me. It twitches with small, sharp breaths, but its nose rasps with fresh blood, and its body hangs limp when I pick it up. Its back is soft, broken.

I ask Child Fly if he thinks this was an accident.

No, he reassures me. *I'm saying you lost control. One minute you had all the pieces in your hand, the next you threw them all up in the air.*

It didn't affect the outcome of the Sacrifice, I tell him. I understood much of what the thought-picture had shown me.

He always has an answer: *But it was incomplete, impure. You didn't see what would happen today, because your observances were imperfect. You deceived yourself, and you knew it, though you didn't understand how. And because you were deceived, you needed to assuage your guilt with an even more powerful ritual later on.*

He can be quite mature, sometimes.

I don't know what to do. I walk over to the canal with the body, offering it to the water. There's no sign from the water, or the wind, or the white clouds in the blue sky; just a twitching bag of loose bones held in my arms. I take the knife from my pocket, flick the blade from its sheath and kneel down. I lower the rabbit gently to the ground and scrape out a circle of flames around me on the baked earth. The wind drops. The black canal is smooth and still. I retreat from the circle, leaving the dying animal behind, watching it. It's almost an hour before it stops breathing.

I press my palm across its back, holding it in place as I perform the rite. Its body is already stiffening. I draw the knife across its throat, expecting spurts of blood to burst free and spray the earth circle; but I already know that the Sacrifice has not been performed correctly, and there's only a smooth, steady ooze of blood from the open wound. Frustrated, I take the knife again, hold the rabbit's foreleg and make a crude, jagged incision, placing the severed paw carefully in my pocket. Then I smear each of my fingers with the blood from the neck and leg, press the wounds against my forehead and along my forearms, and run my fingers across my lips, tasting the blood. The ceremony is almost ended. Taking the corpse in my hand I fling it far out into the middle of the canal, where it splashes and sinks, then resurfaces. The torn, broken corpse floats there, blood seeping from it; a thin, spreading stain.

And as the stain grows it forms an image. At first it means nothing, but then I recognize it. It's the girl on the beach, blood-red flames running along her skin. The flames merge as she grows, becoming deeper and stronger. I see her briefly as she appeared at the disco. Older, standing next to me. And I see my own shape outlined in the blood, sprouting from her side and separating into a new pool on the surface of the water. The two shapes move apart briefly, then change abruptly, following each other at first, then growing together side by side, moving closer. At last the pools merge, intertwining, shapeless. The blood dissipates in the canal.

The message I glimpsed in the castle moat is clear. The ritual is complete. But the Sacrifice has failed, and cannot be repeated.

Child Fly draws the logical conclusion for me: *It was still too tame. Too external. You needed a clean, honest, personal ceremony. You* needed *the Rite of Cutting. It was much more satisfactory, even though it separated us for good. There's nothing like a sharp blade to encourage mental clarity.*

I'm not sure he realizes how *sick* he is.

When my father rang that evening I was still crying for the loss of my rabbit. It wasn't an act: I knew that what I'd done was shameful. Besides, the whole procedure had been futile. After all this time I was *still* looking for an answer. As my mother stroked the scars on my wrists where the rabbit's claws had dug deep, I found it.

The Rite of Cutting was born.

But what about the questions? Didn't anyone miss the rabbit?

You said it had escaped, Child Fly tells me, *while you were cleaning out the hutch – and that you'd tried to catch it. The grief was real enough.*

How do I know he's telling the truth?

I don't.

But I was right about the flame scars on your arm, he says, *and I told you the truth about The Burning. And, if you remember, you began the Cutting after the next vision. You had to register what was happening to you. Permanently. You even said so in your diary.*

There's only one Biscuit left.

But it still doesn't make much sense. Why did I have the thought-pictures in my head even before I was born? Why have they demanded so *many* sacrifices? Why did it have to end like this?

And Child Fly gives the answer he always gives when the supply of Biscuits has run out:

Why are you asking me? I'm only a child.

7

Typical. The past always lets you down in the end – so I'll return to the present. But not to Kate; not yet. Nor to the dinner party. You need to see more of the background first, and I need to perform one of my Rites.

It's time to let you in on a little secret.

There's a Scalpel on the bathroom shelf.

It's one of my five Objects. (When you know about *all* the Objects, you'll understand what happened today a little better.) It's positioned on the left side of the group, because the first Cutting was inscribed on my left hand, and it looks like this: a slim, light, steel handle with a detachable, razor-sharp blade. You can find one like it almost anywhere. I bought mine from an arts and crafts shop about ten years ago, along with five spare blades, vacuum-wrapped in a silver foil packet. I can still see the foil embossed with navy blue letters detailing the make and number; and feel the faint, relieved hiss as the air rushed in when I opened it . . . There are many types of cutting tool, but only scalpels are *pure*.

My own Scalpel is central to the Rite of Cutting. Since I'm about to perform the Rite, here and now, this seems an appropriate time for you to learn about its history and observances – otherwise what I'm about to describe will appear bizarre. It is *not* bizarre. The Rite *must* continue. A new symbol *must* be etched on flesh.

(Don't be alarmed by that sound. I'm only climbing out of the bath to get the Scalpel . . . This room must be the coldest in the bungalow. I've never lived in a house with any kind of fire since I left home. Even the heat from electric bars brings on visions . . . Back in again. That's much better.)

So. I'm holding the Scalpel between the thumb and forefinger of my left hand, as I did all those years ago during the first Rite. I feel now as I did then. With this instrument in my grasp I am artist and canvas, a sculptor of skin, a drawer of blood. I am high priest and sacrifice. I am my own altar. This is not merely a blade: it carries the ceremonial weight of history, the memory of a hundred similar blades, each one cutting flesh, carving its own mark on the past. (These blades are the first part of my Collection. I preserve them in a small box on a high shelf in the garage. Each blade is stained with old, brown blood, and every pattern is different in size, shape and colour. I can name every occasion on which I drew blood, and I know which blade made which mark, where it was done, what it felt like. The results of these Rites can be seen on my skin; my flesh is a coded book, which only I can decipher.)

I stroke the blade. This is the moment of fear and self-loathing, but the procedure is reassuringly formal and well-established. I close my eyes and consider the image I'm about to carve, why it's relevant, and why it *must* be recorded. I don't think about punishment. Nothing but this Scalpel and the patterns it forms can be my accuser, or purge my guilt. Outsiders have no authority to condemn.

I open my eyes and scan the landscape of my skin. Here are the white flames leaping up my left arm to the shoulder: they crackle and spit, and I'm a toddler again drawn to the dancing shadows. There's the white bicycle on my right calf, just below the knee, each wheel with thirteen spokes: they spin into a blur as the bicycle crumples. There's the tall, thin mirror reflecting my father's face from the top of my right thigh: his reptilian eyes watch me when I curl into a foetal position. Here are the fine chains of geometric shapes with exotic names like obscure diseases: *truncated dodecahedron, small rhombicosidodecahedron, rhombicuboctahedron.*

I close my eyes and imagine the photographs. I usually take photos of my wounds when they're fresh. There's a life in new blood which old blood and white scars can't even *suggest*, and I've taken pictures of my Rites almost from the beginning. These photos are the second part of my Collection. I keep them in a large, unmarked cardboard box, arranged in plain brown envelopes by day, month and year. The quality of the prints varies because there have been a number of different cameras, but they're adequate enough. If you want to examine them, the box is kept by the container of blades on the top shelf in the garage.

Now I'm imagining all the scars on my back, from the crude copies of Escher's simpler sketches to household utensils. (The knife is a favourite, but there are tin-openers and forks carved there, too.) These are less accomplished than the carvings on the front. Accuracy is difficult on your back and backside: your hands get twisted all over the place, and the skin's too insensitive. My image of these scars is perfect, but the reality (which I've seen in small mirrors) is a chaos of jagged edges and accidental gashes.

Hang on. I'm assuming too much. Does *any* of this mean anything to you? If I reveal the history of just a few of these carvings, and take you through the Rite of Cutting step by step, perhaps you'll get some idea of its meaning for *me*. This is as it should be. My intention is not to shock. To me, this is not shocking. The brightness of new scars is passionate and angry, and the whiteness of old scars is pure. But both are part of who I am.

This is how it begins. The Scalpel is as long as the distance, on my left hand, from the wrist to the wrinkled little finger. The manufacturer's name has almost faded, but the embossed size is clear. I open the ceremony with these words:

I give this blade to my body; I give my body to this blade. In the moment of their meeting, both skin and steel are one.

I hold the knife above my navel, then rest the sharp edge on my skin. The Cutting is not performed immediately. First, I focus once more on the design I'm about to create (there's no pain in imagination). Next I visualize the layers of dead skin, the deeper tissues and organs, the processes of absorption and excretion. In my mind, I watch the blade slice through the dry dead outer layers, the felted connective tissue and elastic fibres; I watch it pierce the blood vessels, stimulate the nerves, part the fat; I see it poised above thick muscle and white bone. I hardly ever cut as deep as the muscle and have never carved to the bone, but it helps to know the life that lurks beneath the wound. None of us is hollow.

And then it's done. The first incision.

There's no turning back. Flesh is a sack, a protector, a carrier. It can be stitched; it will heal. There's no harm in creating your own, unique skin, in scratching your own patterns on the canvas.

For a brief moment after the cut there's nothing, not even pain. Then there's a sharp, short-lived *sting*. Then a duller wave which overwhelms it.

And then the blood begins to flow.

Blood from the Rites is the third part of my Collection. This part is far from complete, and has always depended on having a container to hand at the time. Even so, I've managed to amass quite an amount over the years: in corked bottles, cans sealed with cling film, plastic tumblers, Tupperware jars, jam jars, old cups, new cups, clear plastic bags, wine glasses, biscuit tins, and a liqueur decanter. According to its age and containment, this blood is congealed, rust-red, red-brown, crusted, powdered, pure, infected, clean or soiled – but in my head it's always as bright as when I first released it. When I *haven't* had a container, I've buried blood, sprayed it on the garden, painted my entire body with it, smeared it on walls and doors, splashed it on windows, brushed it on paper, wiped it on clean towels, emptied it into the toilet, pissed on it, drunk it, sniffed it, left it to dry and scraped off the remnants, rubbed it on my lips, and dyed T-shirts with it. But these actions have only given temporary pleasure; containment brings permanent satisfaction. Once sealed, a container is never opened.

Tonight I'm going to break with tradition. There'll be no saving of blood, and no photographs of the fresh incision. This bath will hold blood, water, flesh and bone. The value of this ceremony will be self-contained: the purity of the moment requires no external record.

The red stain is beginning to cloud the water around my navel, seeping out weakly in a small, nebulous balloon. At the moment it's only a tiny cut, but as I complete the first of the required five designs the volume will increase. This is a gratifying moment and – apart from the permanent record the scar leaves behind – is the most enjoyable part of the ritual. As the gashes heal the surrounding areas generally become sore, particularly in water, but this is the time of highest exultation, made more pleasurable by its brevity.

As I said, the Rite of Cutting began after the rabbit died. The association of its warm, wet blood with the marks its claws had made on my wrist was too powerful a sign to ignore. That evening I sat in my bedroom, trying to interpret the confusion of images and implied messages. Even though I'd washed off the animal blood in the canal I could still smell it, still taste it on my lips, and I saw that only self-mutilation could be personal, direct and clandestine enough a ritual to clarify the thought-pictures. It had the added bonus, too, of recording the important events in my life in a way that wouldn't be forgotten.

I was determined to find the perfect instrument for the first Rite. The first *design* was an obvious choice, and it made the cutting implement equally self-evident. I'd kept the rabbit's foot hidden inside a pair of socks in my wardrobe, and I realized that I could use its claws to carve its own likeness on my body. This method couldn't have been more painful, or less satisfactory. I used the blunt claws to scratch and dig at my skin, to create a pathetic icon of the real thing. A symbol without substance. If I'd preserved the blood from this initial wound the memory might have been easier to bear, but I hadn't yet formulated that part of the ceremony, and there's a small part of my mind which regrets the loss. All that remains of that first Rite is a shapeless, white scar on my left foot.

Before I found the Scalpel, I experimented with many different tools. I was still a little frightened of pain then, and after the failure of the rabbit's foot, I postponed the next Rite for some weeks until my scars healed. The flames from The Burning were the logical next step, and in the end I used a shard of broken glass, taken from a broken bottle dropped in the fireplace. I cleaned it first to avoid infection, but my upper arm was swollen and red for a couple of days after the ceremony, and irritated for about five weeks . . . Also, for every instrument which *did* work there were half a dozen which weren't quite right. Chips of wood (far too painful, too many splinters), household knives (too blunt), a corkscrew (unwieldy), a tenon saw (savage and uncontrollable, a skin-shredder), a wood drill bit (effective but, like the saw, too reminiscent of my father), a pencil sharpener blade (razor sharp, but too small), and paper (gratifyingly painful, but imprecise). All failed. I'm embarrassed that I even *attempted* the Rite with some of these. The pain passes, but the shameful memory is a companion for life. A ceremony demands respect and consistency.

The first of five parts is complete. During the past decade the only words I've been able to think of to celebrate finishing a small section of a larger whole are these:

It is almost done.

And it is. But the simplest designs are often the hardest to draw accurately, and I'm not sure I've been successful with this first attempt. There's *some* resemblance, but . . . Maybe it's the colour. You can never get any colour other than red, of course, but sometimes you can get the shading right, and achieve a balance between the living reds of fresh blood, the liver-browns of dried, and the veal-like white of scars. Watching a scar heal can give your design an animated existence through time which is a wonder to observe . . . I have the shape, I think. A fair compromise between likeness and symbol. This relationship can be disastrously upset if you strive too much for realism, as I've discovered on several occasions. I once tried to recreate Escher's Circle Limit IV on my right buttock, but it was a hopeless mess, and I abandoned it after half a dozen strokes. I've learned to stick to more iconic designs, like cartoons, or tattoos – the whole process is actually quite comparable to both. Reality is nothing. Memory is all.

Anyway, I begin the second part with this oath:

I promise to end what I have begun.

I ended my childhood with the Rite of Cutting. It was a time of change all round. In the same year as the first Rite, my father found a new job (which I still knew nothing about), we moved house, and I changed schools.

School was not a happy place for me. Too many demands, too many empty phrases, too many *words*. And the nicknames! Because of my hands I was known as Felix Burns. Because of the faint white lines on my face I was called Scarface. Most of the time I was just addressed as Buzz. But this is all irrelevant. School was useful for one thing above all else: it gave me the idea for the Scalpel.

There are snatches of conversation you remember all your life, some much more clearly than all the others. I don't understand the reasons. From my primary school I've got a televisual recollection of my headmaster advising us in solemn tones to conserve water. Don't brush your teeth under a running tap. Don't fill the bath above your ankles. And so on. But the snatch of conversation I'm about to repeat is drawn from a biology lesson in secondary school. Here's the scene. I'm watching a rat being dissected. The scalpel blade is clean and cuts easily, and I feel the rough scars of flame and rabbit's foot throbbing on my skin. It's late spring, and a fly enters through an open window, humming, zigzagging, circling, zigzagging, humming.

'Buzz off,' says my friend, David, to the fly. He looks at me and grins. I can see the train reflected in his blue eyes, and those spinning, broken wheels rising high into the air. I can feel the wheels of blood on my right calf, though I haven't even carved them yet.

'Yeah. Buzz *off*,' I repeat.

'All right, Felix, that's enough.' The teacher's bald head reflects a pale image of sunlight and his thin lips frame a warning to us all. 'Settle down.'

The fly describes an erratic orbit around him. Its tiny wings hum. It descends towards the rat. The rat lies on its back with legs splayed and skin clamped apart. Its belly is wide open. The fly hints that, if we all take our hands out of range for a few seconds, it might possibly consider landing on the rat and extending its proboscis to scent the good scents. But we *are* in range, and instead it settles casually on the handle of the scalpel.

Scalpel. Fly.

The link is established. It can't be broken. It's like a weak flash of light, brief and barely noticeable: I am holding the Scalpel and carving my palm.

The fly zigzags through the open window.

*   *   *

The second design is finished. I repeat the oath: *It is almost done.*

This one is more convincing than the first: the long, thin shape curves in a bank of flesh rising from the well of my navel. The colours are acceptable. New blood seeps into the water, now a faint shade of red.

It's a different year, and my mother is bathing me, washing my back with soap and a flannel. I never allowed her to bathe me once I'd begun the Cutting, and at school I disguised the fresh marks with plasters. I avoided sport, of course. Somewhere in space and time there's a huge pile of forged notes full of contrived excuses. And I never went swimming. The water wasn't pure.

I promise to end what I have begun.

The third incision begins. This is deeper than the other two, but I'm still in control. The first wound is already beginning to clot and ache. I move my hands over it, gently easing the thick blood away, smoothing the skin above the waterline, revealing the simple pattern beneath. It's not so bad as I first thought. It's easily recognizable, though anyone who hadn't heard this story to the end might wonder why I decided to create such an unusual image.

Whatever. Let's move on.

I've got bottles of blood, and photographs of blood, I've got Scalpel blades covered in blood . . . and then I have diaries whose pages are smeared with it. These are the fourth part of my Collection, and the last directly concerned with the Rite of Cutting. I call them diaries but they're more like notebooks, recording every Cutting since I bought the Scalpel, and detailing other observations too – such as what I felt about a certain ritual, or my impressions on a particular thought-picture, or what someone said to me that day and why this was Significant. There's one exception: the opening entry in the very first volume. It says something like this:

How do I begin? With the shop – where else?

It's dark, and I feel a bit frightened, but I have to register what's happening to me. There are shelves of paper, bottles of clear and coloured fluids, brushes, easels, chalks, dozens of different pens and pencils, craft kits, wool, palette knives. The shop assistant is quite elderly, late forties perhaps. He doesn't want to talk on equal terms to a child.

Can I help you? he says.

I tell him I'd like a pencil, and smile, but he grimaces back, so I don't smile again.

What kind would you like?

What kinds are there? I'm still cool.

We've got some soft ones, he says, and some hard ones.

He's trying to patronize me because I'm a kid, so I tell him I want a 4B, Medium wash. That fucks him off, and I seize my opportunity, telling him I want an artist's scalpel as well.

Anyway, he gets the pencil first, throws it into a plain white paper bag, and asks: Any particular kind?

I say I need it for cutting card. For a moment he looks suspicious. I'm about to explain that I'm buying it for my father, or give a false address, or simply run away. I'm ready to confess everything about the rabbit, and the Rite, and my thought-pictures. But he says:

I think I've got just the thing. Do you want some blades with it?

And I mumble something and he gets the Scalpel.

I couldn't have made a better choice myself. It's beautiful: slim, silvery, a perfect size and shape. He hands it to me and I try not to look too concerned, too delighted, but I turn it over and over and feel how light it is, how easy to hold, and all the time I'm thinking, It's beautiful, It's beautiful, It's beautiful. There's writing on the handle, and I run my fingers over it. Swann-Morton, BS 2982, B, MADE IN ENGLAND. Size 3. Perfect. Fucking perfect.

Here's the first blood.

I remember smearing blood on the bottom of that page. It's since dried out and flaked off, but there are still some faint brown spots. It was there because I'd been trying to influence the outcome of chiromancy. I was attempting to lengthen my heart, life and love lines with the Scalpel – I felt they were far too short – but I didn't expect the blade to be quite as painful as it was. It looked so smooth and pure that I thought the ceremony would pass cleanly and without distress, but there was a sharp bite, and the handle slipped, and I bisected one of the lines (I don't recall which). Disappointing, but predictable.

Every single entry in each of the five volumes follows the same pattern. There's a description of the ritual, usually followed by a rough drawing of the shape or combination of lines I've carved, and then there's a sample of blood from the ceremony. As I've said, much of the blood is collected and contained, along with the blades; but even when your wounds start to heal there are always patches that need to be mopped up. This is what I smear in the notebooks.

It is almost done.

The third carving ends, the fourth begins. The water is red.

I promise to end what I have begun.

*   *   *

Apart from the volumes detailing the Rites, I've *never* kept a diary. I don't need to – and even if I did, I wouldn't. Diaries are full of self-indulgent half-truths. They don't convey the ideas locked away in your head. And you're always aware of a potential readership: *What will he think if I write that sometimes I want to kill him? And do I mean it anyway?* Your style becomes florid and silly. You sink into dramatic confessions, mixed metaphors, off-the-cuff remarks. You start a process of internal editing, sifting the information to your best advantage. Memories, like this, like now, are naked and alive, not dead records influenced by fashion, or favourite turns of phrase. A diary would lie about this murder.

I did have a *decoy* diary when I was a child. One that I kept hidden under the mattress. It had a few perfunctory entries to make it plausible. You know the kind of thing: *Went out today. Weather good. Bought some things. School's boring. X says he likes Y, but I think Z is in love with both of them.* The bed was the most obvious place to hide it. It's where everyone looks, along with the back of the wardrobe or the underwear drawer. And if they find something, they stop looking for the *real* secret. It worked, too – the ceremonial volumes were protected. I shudder to think what would have happened if my mother had ever found the pages covered in blood . . . Well, I could have waved goodbye to the future. Questions, guilt, misplaced blame. She wouldn't have understood. We shared many good things – a strong relationship and a special bond which I don't have the time or need to describe here – but this was my secret. I couldn't reveal it.

My mother. I can see her now, her oval face shrunk to a scowl, framed by long black hair. There are lines on her skin from laughing too hard. I don't know why she laughed so much. There was nothing amusing about my childhood . . . I see the future in her face. She's asking me *Why? Why did you do it? Was it something we did? What have we done wrong?* And though I try to tell her that it's nothing they've done or said, that the Cutting is just a commemoration, or an interpretation of my visions, the questions continue: *Why? Why? Why?*

Concealment. This whole period before I left home was a tense time of camouflage, and bluff, and privacy. I stored the few bottles and other containers from the early Rites inside the bed. A small incision in the side facing the wall, pulling out the excess stuffing and springs when necessary. My mother never turned the mattress, but even if she had she wouldn't have noticed anything. And I made sure all the containers were sealed with Sellotape and cling film: spots of blood seeping through sheets are a dead give-away. The Scalpel blades – I kept them in a hollowed-out volume of the Gideon Bible, hidden behind a shelf full of cheap horror novels. It was safe enough. Besides, only an idiot puts *all* his private affairs in one place. And the other half of my Collection of Rites mementoes – the ceremonial volumes and the photos of the wounds . . . ? These were both hidden in the attic, inside an old wooden trunk for which I had the only key. The trunk was covered in piles of sheets, soft toys, carpet off-cuts, so it was a laborious process to set up each ceremony and ensure that everything was put back in its proper place. But it was worth it. I was lucky enough to avoid illness, and in the six remaining years I stayed with my parents, they discovered nothing: no scars, no mementoes, not even the time and place of the Rites.

Concealing the scars was not so easy: the greater the number of cuts, the greater the number of excuses needed to avoid suspicion. So I hardly ever wore T-shirts, even in summer; and I insisted on knee-length shorts too, giving any old reason: shy, embarrassed, cold. Teenagers can get away with these kind of lies. Parents expect their children to turn into sullen, reclusive, inarticulate morons, and I was just fulfilling a role. It became simpler as I grew older. If I'd discovered the Cutting earlier it wouldn't have been so straightforward.

The fourth ends, the fifth begins. The water is red, the skin stings. *It is almost done. I promise to end what I have begun.*

Was I an abnormal child? Of course. Was my life one long misery of self-abuse and mutilation and symbol? No. Most of the time I was happy and stable enough; but – be honest – we all have parts of us that we'd rather keep hidden, even from our closest friends. My secrets were no more special than yours. Just a little more eccentric, maybe. My life hasn't been all flesh and blood: it's just that I get moments when I need to know what the pictures are trying to tell me. You have to adapt to cope, and the Rite of Cutting has been my way of coping. If I highlight these rituals now it's because they play a dominant part in this story; but, really, they're just one of many intertwined threads leading to the present. They've been selected because they're also those threads that led to the killing.

One final thought:

I have, during some ceremonies, tasted my own blood. We've all done it. Everyone recognizes that thick, salty, meaty flavour. If you *haven't* tasted it, what are you afraid of? If you bleed, you should consume. It's a . . . waste, a blasphemy to watch it spill onto concrete and carpet and earth. Take the liquid from the wound, as I do now, pass it onto your tongue, feel the *life*.

*　　*　　*

It is done. Skin and steel are no longer one, and I have ended what I began. I offer this blood, this blade, and this cut flesh to the past, present and future.

I've just removed the blade from the final patch of skin. The incisions are complete, the Rite almost ended. If you carve, don't carve idly. Cutting flesh is a skill. No . . . It's an *art*, whether the flesh be animal or human. Blood is the stuff of magic and myth, and it shouldn't simply be accepted, or blindly feared, but *cherished*.

Each of the five shapes I've created is different, but they all describe the same basic pattern. There are variations in depth and style, in the angle at which the Scalpel blade was held, in the amount of blood released – but as a connected whole they represent the accident and purpose behind tonight's events. A permanent wound. Serious. Absurd. Memorable.

This is the pattern. Arranged around my navel are five self-contained incisions, each one inseparable from the whole design:

A pentagon of sausages.

8

Talking of sausages, it's time I introduced my second friend: Allan. Al for short. Big Al when we want to annoy him.

I've known him for three years. He used to work on the production line in a sausage factory, which is where I met him, but eventually slithered his way up the corporate ladder to the sales department. Not that it matters. He doesn't work there anymore. Anyway, the point is, he usually avoids eating sausages in any shape. If you ever find yourself grilling or frying a couple of polonies for him at some dinner party, don't try to disguise them. He won't be fooled. *I know what goes in them*, he'll say, *and I won't eat them*. (It used to be a joke between Sue and me that he got so big – Al is *very* fat – because he ate all the sausages he oversaw. OK. So it's *not* funny.) He once told us what they put in the sausages where he worked: powdered bone, shredded pork, miscellaneous animal fat, bread or rusk, water, sheep bits (for the casings), any seasoning that came to hand, and – get this – all the scrag ends that no one wanted, such as the glands and kernels from the pig's cheeks, eyeballs, and whatever else anyone could find on the factory floor. *They just chucked it all in*, he says. (I don't know whether to believe him. John and I make all our own sausages at work now, so obviously *our* ingredients are more wholesome. In fact, I'll be revealing some sausage-making tips near the end of this story.) But here's the other point. Tonight, Al made an exception to his own rule: like everyone else, apart from me, he ate one of *my* sausages.

OK. The accident. Al's centre of gravity has never been what it ought. Nor has his choice in bicycles. He was two stones heavier and four years younger when this incident happened, and he's never ridden a bike since. He was cycling home one evening with two shopping bags hanging from the handlebars. It was windy, but everything was OK until he approached a roundabout, where a lorry squeezed him into the kerb. The bags started swinging, he overcompensated, the shopping got caught in the spokes and – this is the part that makes me think Al is cursed – the handlebars came off in his hands. He says he continued in an upright position for a few more seconds before the weight of the shopping and his lack of natural balance sent him earthward . . . Anyway, the next day he took the bike back to the shop where he'd bought it. They said they couldn't help him until the manager came back. He suggested leaving the bike with them, without securing a receipt, and they agreed. When he came back the day after, they denied any knowledge of him *or* his bicycle. Some people are like that.

9

Bicycles, incidentally, always make me think of David. David was my best friend at secondary school, and what happened to him is connected with all sorts of Rites and Symbols and Objects, so this is as good a time as any to tell you his story.

There are a couple of things you should know about him before I begin. He was the first person to call me Lucky – I think he just stumbled across my name in a dictionary; no one else caught on till much later, so it was like a shared secret, just between *us* – and he taught me two lessons I've never forgotten. The first was the value of skin: this gave me the idea for the Rite of Exposure. The second was the stupidity of taking the game too far – as you're about to hear. In return, he was the only person with whom I shared the mysteries of the Rite of Cutting. Until last night, of course.

I was thinking about him on Thursday, the night *before* last – and I might as well start there. I always think about him when I talk to my friends; and I'd been calling them about the dinner party. (They all accepted my invitation, of course. I may not be much of a conversationalist, but they like a free feed.) Anyway, as soon as I'd made the last call, David spoke to me:

'Are you *chicken*?' he said.

He was standing on the brow of the hill, looking down at the level-crossing. The barriers were lowering and a warning bell was ringing distantly. Twin amber lights at the track side flashed alternately, on, off, on, off. I fingered the knife in my pocket, wondering what to say. I couldn't tell him what I knew, so I looked at him with my mouth open, like a beached fish, and said nothing. I said *nothing*, when I should have told him everything. I knew this hesitation was all part of the process, but every thought I had, and every moment we wasted, just tightened the noose. He stood there trying to persuade me, to dare me, and all the while the future was rushing to meet him.

'All right, then. If *you* won't do it, I will. But you're going to owe me. After this, I'm the King of Dare.'

He swung his leg over the bar, pushed his feet off the ground, sat forward in the saddle, and pedalled downhill. I thought it might happen in slow motion, as it always had in the visions, but he picked up speed as he descended, the bicycle wheels spinning, his feet whirling on the pedals, body arced forward, hurtling towards the barriers.

And I was so afraid, so alone.

But the story starts before this, when David said:
'D'you fancy going leech-hunting?'

83

We were on the telephone. It was the first Monday morning of the summer holidays, and he was keen to celebrate his freedom. 'We can stop at the dam on the way. Build a bigger sluice gate, pile on the mud. We could make a lake.'

We'd built the dam the previous afternoon, and it was already very big. We were both praying that no rival gang had come along and destroyed it overnight. But we'd built it in the woods, in a deep hollow bordered by rocks and high walls of soft mud. You had to seek it out if you were to have a hope of finding it.

'OK,' I agreed. Even if I'd said no, I doubt I could have prevented the sequence of events that would lead to him cycling away from me, down towards the railway track. I turned the rabbit's foot over and over in my back pocket. It always seemed to be with me now. 'And guess what?' I boasted.

'What?'

'I've found out what a human brain looks like.'

'Tell me when we get to the dam. Meet me in about half an hour. Bring your knife for the leeches – and don't forget your bike.'

When I arrived he was already on guard, armed with a catapult and a handful of stones. I saw him before he saw me, and gave the signal to approach: two bird-whistles. I left the bike half-concealed behind a thicket and scrambled down the steep slope to a level patch of ground. The dam was still mostly intact, though the water itself had loosened some earth along the rough sluice channel, lowering the level of the lake. Even so, it was an impressive sight to see David dwarfed on the far side of the earth wall. I edged around the side of the stream and joined him.

'No one's been near it yet,' he said. He looked at our

construction work with obvious pride, then listened to a faint cracking sound in the distance, holding his hand against my mouth and hissing for me to keep quiet. I admired his hands. They were rough and small, but immensely strong. He could shift great piles of clay or sludge in a single scoop. He had power over me and realized it – not just then, but for as long as we'd known each other. But he never abused it. I even believed that he had some respect for me in return . . . Anyway, the sound proved to be a false alarm. 'Let's get a move on,' he said. 'I reckon we should add a couple of feet here, then ride over to the canal and bag some leeches. I've brought a can.'

He was no taller than me, but he filled his clothes more easily. His skin always seemed to be well tanned, too – at least that's how I remember it – and I almost always see him now in a plain white T-shirt and blue jeans, hardly ever in school uniform. His eyes were blue, like the sea on a hot summer's day, and his hair was blond like the beach, and his body was pure, untainted by scars. I don't know if I *loved* him. There was an unspoken bond between us, an invisible contract which couldn't be broken. A few of the girls in our class made it obvious they had a crush on him, but he chose me. You grow older, it all changes, you move apart – but there are times and places when friendship is perfect.

'So tell me about the brain.'

We were scraping mud and small stones from the walls of the hollow, clouding the lake and losing a lot of the earth to the water. But little by little the dam wall was rising higher. We created a gap on the right side so that the pressure wouldn't build up too early, but there was a boulder just the correct weight and shape to fill it, and we'd already dug out the sluice in the opposite bank, sealed with a piece of wood and the pressure of the stream.

'I saw it on TV,' I told him. 'It's this *huge* thing, like a knobbly potato made out of putty. It's full of nerves and veins, and different bits of the potato allow you to see and think and feel.'

He was unimpressed, and scooped a mound of gravel onto the back of the dam, reinforcing the wall. Like many of the things he did, it was something I hadn't thought of.

'I've seen one in books,' he said, 'and that looked like a load of blue and red wires, all bunched together like a hair ball.' He glanced at me, then grabbed hold of a boulder the length of his forearm. 'Tell you what. Let's have a look inside *your* head and find out.' He drew the stone high into the air above his head, and for a moment I thought he really was going to drop it onto my skull.

(Well – all things considered – it wouldn't have been a bad time to die.)

But instead he threw it into the small lake, where it sank like – well, like a stone – and the water sprayed high in the air, soaking me from head to toe, and sent huge tidal waves cascading over the top of the dam, wiping out the entire civilian population in the valley below. He started to laugh uncontrollably, and didn't see the missile of wet mud homing in on his chest. He stopped laughing, looked confused for a moment, and then retaliated with another shower of water, this time the result of a well-directed boot. His boots were always black, I remember. After a few more exchanges we regained control, came to an informal truce, and got on with the building.

Now that we were already dirty there was no stopping us. We felt less inhibited about the work and continued without another word. It was hot by the time we'd finished the main arc wall. We opened the wooden sluice on the left completely, and sealed the gap on the right with the boulder, filling in the smaller holes with a layer of gravel and mud on the water side, and a layer of packed earth on the dry side. Finally, we stood back and scrutinized our handiwork, as all builders do, patching up the dribbles and rivulets with more stones and mud, and propping up vulnerable areas with piles of rocks and twigs. It looked crude and unprofessional, but it was effective.

When we lowered the sluice gate again the lake began to fill. This is always a nervous moment for the dam-builder, and we had to judge the strength of the stream and adjust the opening accordingly. The gate was David's idea: he'd found a piece of bark in the woods which had gone a bit rotten, but was still robust enough to hold back the flow. He had a knack for finding useful things . . . We crouched on the bank of the stream, watching the lake fill, admiring what we'd achieved. We were both caked in mud, which was beginning to crack and flake, gripping the skin beneath it.

It was getting hotter.

I'd known him since before the Rite of Cutting began. When we first met I knew straightaway that he was the rider of the bicycle: he had the train in his eyes even then. And his skin was so pure . . . I *wanted* that skin. I wanted to cut our names in it with my pen-knife. I wanted to carve him as he lay down before me, wanting to be carved; and to draw blood from him gently, and to worship his purity. But his skin was untouched, and that increased its value infinitely. (Don't misunderstand me. I didn't want to harm him. I wanted him to desire the Cutting, as I desired it. Otherwise it would just have been a violation. An assault.)

I think he knew about my scars before that day at the dam. Until then he never asked why I wouldn't go swimming, why

I covered parts of my skin when we played football. But I think he knew. He never saw me cut myself – no one did – so he must have thought that I'd been in some accident which I couldn't talk about, or my parents were violent, or I was just some weirdo who liked wearing large plasters.

So it was no surprise when he asked: 'What happened to your arm?'

We'd left the dam and returned to The Den, an upturned oil tank, shaped like a cube, with small holes in the side to let in the light, and a doorway bent and ripped outwards from the thin, rusting metal. It still smelled of oil, like the surrounding grass. (The Den was something else David had found. It was at the far end of the field behind my house, strictly on private property, but once you'd sneaked inside nobody could tell you were there. It was where he came to smoke, and where we exchanged knowledge about life, death and the sexual experiences of the Milky Bar Kid.)

When I didn't answer, he repeated the question. He thought I hadn't heard him, but I was wondering what to say. One of the plasters had got wet and was pulling away from the skin, revealing a pinkish, triangular scar. The beginning of the first tongue of flame.

'Nothing. Just a cut.'

'Must be a big cut.' He wasn't going to let it drop. He wasn't the kind of friend who would leap at me, pin me down, and rip off the plaster, but he had other, subtler ways of removing it.

'It is. It was an accident.'

It was dark inside The Den, and I could barely see the skin on his forehead, let alone his deep blue eyes. It would be clearer in a couple of minutes, when we got used to the light.

'What kind of accident? Have you been in a fight?' A slight pause. I saw his eyes at last. 'What?'

'Just an accident. You know.'

My heart was pounding rapidly. I was sure he could hear it. It sounded like a gorilla beating its chest. I wanted to tell him, but I didn't want to tell him, but I wanted to tell him. I couldn't tell him. I should. It was the last big secret between us, and there were no big secrets. *Ask me again*. And what did it matter anyway, after today? He wouldn't go around shouting it to everyone he met. My friend's a nutter. My friend's a *fucking* nutter. He wouldn't. My friend's a fucking nutter and he should be locked up.

'Are you trying to scare me?' He was getting nervous. "Cos I'm not scared." He stared at me with his golden skin covered in mud. 'But, look, if it's a big deal we'll forget about it.'

'It's not a big deal.' I began to feel sick. The smell of oil in my nostrils, rich, thick, like blood.

'Then stop pissing about and tell me.'

I thought about it, and thought again, and I saw his eyes reflecting the sky and the train, and I said, 'All right then.' He smiled and nodded, satisfied. 'But you'll have to promise me that you won't tell anyone.' I pulled out my pocket knife. 'On your mum's life.'

'Yeah, yeah, I promise.'

'I *mean* it,' I warned. 'If anyone finds out about this they'll . . . I don't *know* what'll happen.'

'Kill me, carve me up, and dance on my bones if I tell a soul.'

So I told him. I told him about The Burning, and the girl on the beach, and the rabbit. It wasn't the whole truth. Somewhere between sharing the secret and regretting its loss, my defences went up and I said that my cuts were just preventative magic against future accidents. It was easy to do. And I didn't tell him about the thought-pictures. Except for the important one:

'It's confusing. I can see you riding down a hill towards the railway, and then there's a spinning wheel, and I don't know what's happening, but I don't think it's good.' I knew the exact sequence of events, of course. Frame by frame. I could wind them backwards and forwards in my head. Unlike many of my visions, there was nothing cryptic about the message here. It would happen.

And, perhaps, some small part of me wanted it to.

'You probably just dreamt it,' he reassured me, squinting through one of the small holes in the metal wall. 'It's a bit creepy, though.'

'I don't think it was a dream. It's not *like* that. It's—'

'I'll tell you what,' he interrupted, 'We'll bike up to the hill above the railway crossing after we've been to the canal, and I'll prove to you it *was* just a dream.' He started waving his hands around agitatedly. 'Anyway, it's stupid to think that you can tell what's going to happen before it does.' He banged his head hard on the roof, deliberately; there was a loud, reverberating clang. 'See? Did you expect me to do that?' I laughed, and shook my head. 'No, 'course you didn't. I've had dreams like yours as well, and it never happens the way you see it. You can change the future any time you want.'

The route to the canal was the same one I'd followed with the rabbit cradled in my arms. It's only about a mile. There's an open rubbish dump on this side of the hill now, but when *we* were there it was all rough grassland. It was hard work pushing the bikes up the slope, and terrifying juddering down the other side – I almost crashed straight into the canal. We cycled along the towpath to the railway bridge, then crossed over. At the far side we left the bikes under the arch, David removed an empty tomato soup can from his saddle-bag, and we walked along the bank, knives at the ready. The waterway was derelict even then. Most of the bank was reinforced with sheet pile wall, red with rust. In places it had disappeared altogether. Plants had pushed the concrete and metal aside and destroyed large areas of the towpath. But the crevices and smooth, algae-covered banks were a perfect home for leeches.

I let out the first cry of triumph. A leech was clinging to the wall just below the waterline, undulating slowly upwards. It was like a soft, tiny skittle, with ribbed, black, slippery flesh. I leaned over the edge and stretched for it with my hand, then checked myself. Leeches are surprisingly easy to pull off, but if you haven't got a firm hold, they can slither out of your grasp just as quickly. I stabbed it with the point of the knife instead, scraping it up until I could grab hold of its fat, rubbery body. I held it between blade and fingers until David came along with the can, then dropped it in. It writhed around sluggishly, and I watched it suffer for a while.

When I looked up David was staring at my left arm. I followed his gaze and saw that the big plaster was hanging loose, exposing not just the first triangular tongue of flame but a huge, curling column of fire. I reached over to put it back, but he stopped me with his hand.

'No.' He seemed to be framing his words. 'Can I see it?'

I nodded. I could see he was fascinated, and I was flattered that he was interested in me and wanted to know more. I rolled back my shirt sleeve to the shoulder, and peeled off the plasters, slowly, watching him all the time, watching his eyes widen and his pupils dilate. The rectangular patch of skin beneath was whiter than the rest of my body and bordered by traces of grimy adhesive. A dozen thick, pale pink scars curled around my upper arm.

'Ugh,' he said. 'It's horrible.'

I knew he didn't mean it, and his fascination pleased me. The scars were raised in little ridges, coiling and writhing along the flesh. I could smell my tiny hands burning, hear the crackling of the flames, feel the pain on my face, see the flesh melting like wax, taste the bitter smoke. I flexed my muscles to show him how the fire could come alive, and he stepped back, grimacing – but returned again, peering closely.

'Can I touch it?'

I agreed. He crouched down beside me and ran his rough, dry-mud fingers over the old wound. He was so careful, so gentle. Much later, when Kate caressed that arm with her fingers, I was dragged back in time to that moment by the canal, and had to pull away from her. But that's another story.

Then came the questions, rapidly, one after the other:

Does it hurt? No.

What did you use? A broken bottle.

Did it hurt when you did it? Yes.

Why did you do it? Silence.

Why did you do it?

'I told you before. It's protection against the future.'

'But you were fibbing. I know you were.'

I paused. How did he know?

'OK . . . But you can't tell anyone.'

''Course not.'

'Well, it's like this. It's like a record. I need a record of what's happened to me. Only the major events.' I tried to be flippant. 'It's better than a diary, but the ink dries a lot more slowly.'

'Uh-huh.'

'And it helps me understand the dream I told you about. I don't know how. It's just that the pain gets rid of the static. It lets my attention focus completely on the vision. Clears up the images. Sorts them out.'

He touched the deeper wounds nearer the shoulder, first with his forefinger then, individually, his middle finger, ring finger, and little finger. But he asked no more questions, and after giving me a brief look of puzzlement, he stood up and said, simply: 'Let's go and catch some more leeches.'

So we did, and this time we stuck closer together. The sun was already falling when we'd filled the can. There must have been two dozen leeches in there. Some dead, most slithering slowly. And I realized there was a big question looming: *What were we going to do with them?*

David answered it. 'OK,' he announced, sitting down and placing the can between us, 'It's Dare time.'

I've never really abandoned Dare. I thought about it tonight, while I was cooking. Wasn't today just one *big* Dare? Wasn't I seeing if I could push myself to do it? (And I did – so perhaps *I'm* the king, after all).

If anything, the stakes were higher back then, because we had less sense of danger. We devised new Dares for each other all the time, each one a little more dangerous and demanding. It began as an anti-social thing – knocking on people's doors and running away, stealing through gardens, throwing rocks at greenhouses – but mutated into something more testing. We did all the usual stuff like jumping off bridges into the canal, climbing on factory roofs, and getting as close as possible to bonfires, but the worst of all was the Traffic Dare.

It was one of David's ideas, and it should have warned me that he could push the game too far. I remember dressing totally in black. Black balaclava, gloves, and scarf, too. And then we headed for the ring road, late at night. About ten, I think. When we saw a clear patch in the traffic, we ran into the middle of the carriageway and lay down on our backs, with our heads pointing towards the cars so that we couldn't see what was coming. It was a game of chicken: the one who ran first was the loser. And it went on for a few nights – four or five, maybe. At first we were relaxed about it, standing up, brushing down our clothes, stretching, yawning, and always leaving plenty of time to stroll away from danger. But as the days went by we gradually left less opportunity to run, until the vision I saw in David's eyes changed from a deep blue sky and a train to a black night and car headlights.

I conceded the Dare.

Back to the canal.

David picked up a leech, holding it (with difficulty) between thumb and forefinger. 'If you can put two of these on your forearm for thirty seconds, I'll get my pen-knife and cut a short, straight line *here*.' He lifted his T-shirt and pointed to his chest. *That* was why he'd been quiet as we walked along. He'd been thinking about the stakes.

'I've got a better idea,' I told him. 'If I put *five* leeches on my arm, let *me* cut you. It doesn't have to be deep. And I know more about it.'

'You're on.'

If he thought before agreeing, it didn't show. Maybe he was just curious. Maybe he wanted to know what it felt like. But he didn't really have any choice: five, as anyone accustomed to the strict rules of Dare knows, is a number that cannot be refused.

Some people loathe invertebrates. I don't. Give me a garden

full of slugs, and snails, and worms, and throw in a couple of cephalopods for good measure – I won't bat an eyelid. So it didn't bother me: digging my fingers deep inside the can and sliding out one leech after another. I lined them evenly across my left arm, from the elbow to the rabbit claw marks, and let them get on with it. I'd read somewhere that they anaesthetized the area they sucked, so I wasn't expecting the prickling sensation; but it soon passed. Anyway, the half-minute lasted far longer than I expected, partly because David was timing it and cheating, but also because I felt more and more nauseous as the time went on. In the end I was grateful to pull them off and chuck them on the bank. When I looked at my arm, it was covered in sore, red, leech-shaped patches. And a couple of spots of blood, which I spread out to make one long, thin stain. I had a blinding vision of squeezing a leech until it burst.

'Your turn.'

'How d'you start?' he asked. It took me a moment to realize that he didn't simply want to be cut. He wanted the Rite that went with it.

'I've just bought a Scalpel, but I haven't got it with me. You could have used that. But I've used lots of other things, so it doesn't really matter.' The memory comes alive. I see myself using the Scalpel to carve the bicycle: the two wheels, each with thirteen spokes, the bent handlebars, the broken frame, the crushed seat. 'Why don't we use your pen-knife?'

'Will it be sharp enough?' He seems apprehensive. I've *never* seen him like this. It makes me feel powerful.

'You should know.' He gives me the knife, and I flick open the blade, holding it between us at eye level. 'Lift up your T-shirt.' He rolls it up to the neck. His hands are clenched into fists. 'Is there anything you want to say?'

'Like what?'

'Anything you want. You know . . . Why do you want to be cut? What do you think you'll feel?'

'I don't want to say anything.'

'Then say nothing.' I turn the blade flat, upright, sideways, then rest it on the skin of his chest. He breathes in sharply because the metal's cold. 'How long d'you want it to be?'

'You decide.'

I rest the point over his left nipple, then turn the blade and push inwards. Quickly, and without fuss, I pull it two inches across his perfect skin. He lets out a sharp cry and jerks backwards, almost falling over.

'I'm sorry. I didn't—'

'It's all right,' he interrupts.

I wipe the knife on the grass before folding it and handing it back to him. His beautiful skin has been defiled – but he doesn't seem to mind. There's bright blood seeping from his shallow wound, and he smooths it around his left nipple, then down to his belly. His hand is shaking. After a few minutes, the flow stops, and there are congealed globules dotted around the cut.

'I didn't mean to . . . I mean, I didn't want it to hurt.'

'It's OK,' he repeats. 'But I don't think I'll do it again.'

He smiles at me; but there's fear in there, too.

After the wound had dried, we walked back along the towpath to the bridge. David sealed the can of leeches with his handkerchief and an elastic band, then packed it into his saddlebag.

'Now for your stupid dream,' he said.

We pushed the bikes back over the bridge and half-carried, half-pushed them up the hill toward the two-lane road heading out of town. We were both tired when we reached the top. I was feeling a bit sick after the leeches, and I think he felt a mixture of confusion and shock. I promised myself then that no one else would ever find out about the Cutting, and that however close I was to my friends in the future, I wouldn't invite them into the Rite. Cutting was a need, not a desire.

(I kept the promise until today. Almost a decade.)

We're almost there now.

At the top of the hill there's a snake. A smooth, black serpent of tarmac, slithering away from us for about half a mile, sliding gently down to the level-crossing. The barriers are raised.

(I feel the rumbling of the train, but there's no train coming.)

'Look,' I tell him. 'This is stupid. Let's go home.'

'I'll just stay a couple of minutes.' He doesn't move, but watches the upright barriers, waiting for them to close. He turns to me briefly. 'Is this the hill, like it was in your dream?'

'No. It was different somehow.' I'm lying, and he knows it, and I lose control. 'Look, I'm fed up with this. I'm knackered and I want to get back before dark. We haven't got any lights.'

He thinks for a moment, then his shoulders drop, and he turns around in resignation. 'OK, then. There's no train coming anyway.'

The warning bell sounds, the lights flash, the barriers begin to fall.

David's body stiffens, and he whirls round again, holding the handlebars toward the crossing. 'Are you coming?' I shake my head. 'What's the matter? You don't seriously think . . . ?' His mouth breaks into a smile. 'Are you *chicken*?' Twin amber lights at either side of the track flash alternately, on, off, on, off. I finger the knife in my pocket, and say nothing. 'All right, then. If *you* won't do it, I will. But you're going to owe me. After this, I'm the King of Dare.'

And he rolls away gently at first, then starts to pedal, then falls away from me on the back of the tarmac snake, his bicycle wheels spinning faster and faster like magical golden coins, like twin stars.

I feel the train approaching.

It's so distant and faint that I want to disbelieve it. But after the juddering there's a quiet rumbling, growing steadily louder, and a high-pitched rhythmic roar. The train is casual at first. It doesn't want to arrive. It can wait until he rides safely over. But as he hurtles closer to the barriers, there is interest, then eagerness, then cartoon malice as the thundering metal engine thrusts its way through the hills and screams into view.

David is almost at the crossing, and he, too, can see the train. He hesitates, stops pedalling, slows for a moment. He's too far away for me to tell whether he thinks he can't make it and is about to stop, or he's still committing himself to the Dare. Stupid.

He pedals again, and picks up speed.

This memory is now so clear that I can't distinguish reality from thought-picture. I leap onto my bike and chase pathetically after him, calling (but he can't hear), warning (but he can't hear), riding as quickly as I can (but it's already too late). He might make it, he could still pull up short—

I was halfway down the hill when he swerved around the barrier and the train hit him. It looked for a moment as if he'd get away with it. He was trying to jump off before he collided; his hands had left the bars and he was leaning back. I didn't hear him cry out; the deep warning siren from the engine drowned all sound. The train brushed him aside indifferently, a hand swatting a fly, tossing him low over the boundary fence and onto the hillside.

Long before the shrieking of the engine's brakes had ceased, I was standing next to his broken body. His bicycle was some way ahead, the frame snapped in two, the seat squashed, the handlebars twisted at a crazy angle. The wheels were nowhere to be seen.

It was the first time I'd seen a dead body. I expected him to wake up and call me an idiot for thinking he'd been hurt. He still had colour in his battered cheeks. I sat next to him and put my hands on his chest. It was the only part of him that was unscathed and unbloodied: his head had been bashed in, his legs were crushed, one of his arms was almost torn off. I'd seen it all before in my head, of course – but I'd censored these details. Did that make me accountable? Did I really *want* it to happen? Desire is a terrible emotion. If you yield to it, you have to take responsibility for the consequences.

But even if I was to blame, what I saw still shocked me. It was a violation of his skin. His beautiful, valuable, uncut skin.

A new thought-picture shook me. I took the rabbit's foot from my back pocket and placed it gently on his chest, below the breastbone. I reached into my front pocket for my knife and flicked the blade open. I had to work quickly. I rested the point just above the right nipple and made a deep, continuous incision around an unmarked patch of skin. Warm blood spread across his chest and over my hands, soaking the rabbit's foot. I turned the knife flatways and began to slice, backwards and forwards, to free the small oblong of flesh. It was hard work. When it was done, I scraped off the blood and pieces of loose fat, and stuffed the Skin into my back pocket; then I folded the knife and pocketed that, too. (The Skin is now the

Second Object. It lies on the opposite end of the shelf from the Scalpel. One side is slightly charred.) Then I wiped the excess blood from the rabbit's foot and, holding it between thumb and forefinger, arranged it in the centre of the open wound.

Foot for flesh. It was a fair exchange. I hope you can see that.

There were people looking through the windows of the train in the distance, and others approaching, still some way off. I cleaned my hands on the grass, turned, and ran to the bike. I was some distance away by the time they reached the body, and I wasn't afraid that they might have recognized me.

I hadn't foreseen it.

On the way back home I saw David again. He was calling me from the bottom of the hollow above the dam. 'Lucky!' he shouted; and I laughed. I broke off from the road and pushed the bike into the woods, hiding it once again in the thicket, and scrambling down the slope. He wasn't there, of course, but the dam was still intact, the sluice gate still holding.

It was almost nightfall, and the lake was in complete shadow. I could just see enough to sit astride the crest of the dam and begin cutting the image of the bicycle, on my left calf, just below the knee. It didn't take long, though it was tricky carving each of the twenty-six spokes, and the bent seat looked more like a kidney. There was no real pain, and the blood disappeared in the lake, fading from a thick black cloud to a thin grey eel, sucked down through the sluice to the far side of the earth wall.

It was cold and dark when I decided to go home. Explanations would be needed, but I was the king of lies, and it didn't worry me. There was still one last act to be performed, though. I stood in the lake with the water running over my thighs and pushed the dam outwards with my feet and arms, until it began to break. It didn't take much; perhaps it hadn't been so strong after all. As the water flooded through the gap and pushed aside even more of the wall we'd made, I felt an immense sense of satisfaction and relief.

And since then, the whirling, magical wheels of his broken bicycle have never stopped spinning.

10

Is this confusing? I'm sorry if it is. I've got this coherent, linear narrative in my head, but the memories keep pushing me backwards and forwards in time. The thing is, all the events are wrapped around each other, and everything is inter-connected, and sometimes there are just too many links to choose from.

Well, that's *my* excuse.

I'll make it easier for you: I've told you about two of the five Objects (the Scalpel and David's Skin), three of the five Symbols (the flame, the rabbit's foot and the bicycle), and four-fifths of my Collection (the stored remnants of the Rite of Cutting). In the next few minutes I'll reveal the final part of the Collection. (If you've forgotten the other four parts, rewind the tape – it was only about twenty minutes ago. And while you're here, GET A GRIP.) After that, I'll tell you about the last two Symbols. In the meantime, forget about the final three Objects: they won't appear until the last section of this story.

Symbol number four, in case you can't remember, is an erect penis. Don't get too excited. It's really nothing special.

Well, maybe it is. Judge for yourself.

But not yet. First, I'll put my fingers around the throat of this story and squeeze hard until it begins at the beginning and tells you what happened yesterday lunchtime.

I was standing outside Pizza Express waiting for Kate. I'd been working in the market all morning, and I hadn't been able to stop thinking about David. (I'd been reminded of him the night before, if you recall, when I telephoned all my friends to invite them to the dinner party.) And I saw his bicycle wheels everywhere: in circular cross-sections of bone, in whirls of minced meat, in the waste offal bin, in the revolving blade of the bacon slicer, in gammon hocks, in the eyes of dead animals, and so on. Even when I looked outside, all I seemed to see were Cheddar truckles, beer barrels, Danish pastries, milk bottles, display cartwheels, and round signs. Round *signs*, for God's sake.

But that's enough. You get the idea.

I think I knew then that Kate would be connected in some way to one of the killings; perhaps even to both. The thought-picture was becoming clearer by the hour. I didn't know whether she'd be the victim, or the one who'd find me standing over the corpse, or if she'd just be the person who drove me to the scene of the crime, handed me the knife, and said, 'From this time/Such I account thy love.' (That's Shakespeare, from what I can remember.) Anyway, I decided I'd need to have a Rite of Cutting that evening to clarify the situation.

Well, I know *now* how all the pieces fit together. And, if you'll forgive the cliché, it's not a pretty picture.

I was standing outside the restaurant for ten minutes before she came. If I hadn't waited those ten minutes, I wouldn't have had time to think about our relationship (more about that later), and I wouldn't have had that blinding vision of the pentagon of sausages which, as you know, is currently inscribed around my navel. That patch of skin is burning like *fuck* now – but it's all part of the fun.

So I had the vision of the sausages, and suddenly I didn't feel so hungry. I've been relatively free of thought-pictures for the last couple of years. Because of Kate, I'd even convinced myself they were finished for good; until the last few days I'd hardly had any. The frequency of Rites of Exposure had increased, of course, but the visions appeared rarely. And when they *did* strike they were brief and violent, with the quaint side-effect of temporarily obliterating the rest of the world.

Anyway, she arrived eventually. I'll try to give you an impression of her voice – it goes something like this:

'Felix?' she said. She drew me out of the trance, and asked if I was OK. I was. You don't begin confessing your entire history of hallucination and ritual self-abuse when you've got to get back to work by one o'clock.

'Sorry I'm late,' she said.

''Salright,' I replied. Exactly that contraction: *'Salright*.

'I'm starving. Are you?'

'Sort of . . . Yeah.'

She tutted, and made some comment about my lack of enthusiasm, and we climbed the winding stair to pizza heaven in silence. At the top we were greeted by a skinny young waiter dressed entirely in black and white: penguin-black shoes, angel-white socks, coal-black trousers, ivory-white shirt, seal-black waistcoat, swan-white neck, beetle-black bow-tie, ferret-white face, oil-black hair. He looked like a zebra-crossing, and I would have told him so, but the opportunity never arose.

'For two?' he said.

His tone was a shade below patronizing and a shade above servile, but I ignored it with a combination of mock aloofness and pseudo-deference. (As you do.)

'Yeah,' I said. 'Smoking.'

He led us to a small table with two chairs, one facing the window, the other facing outwards towards the restaurant. I chose the latter and sat down. The waiter brought two menus and shuffled away to the kitchen.

'So how's work?' I asked.

'Same as ever. How's yours?'

I shrugged. 'Usual.' Then, for a reason which still eludes me, I confessed the first of my secrets. 'Oh, I dunno . . . I keep wanting to do something . . . *different*, you know? Something *exciting*. Like, um . . . juggling a bunch of pigs' kidneys, right in front of the customers.' I mimicked the action with my hands. 'I don't think John would appreciate it, though.' She snorted, and I became slightly embarrassed and started fiddling with the pepper grinder. 'But who knows? He's a cool kinda guy.'

'*Cool* is so out-of-date.'

'Yeah, yeah. Whatever.'

During this exchange – bear with me on this – I could see something *wriggling* inside her, just below the skin; something beneath the creases in her forehead. It was some vile worm, some slimy length of living matter. And it bothered her. It bothered her so much that, after a brief silence, she just had to deal with it, right there and then:

'Look, I know this is a bit abrupt, but can I ask you something?'

'Uh-huh.'

'It's no big deal, but . . .'

'Anything. Yeah.' I spread my palms wide, but I thought: *Do I know her? Can I trust her?*

'I don't know how to . . .' Her face twisted with concern, and the worm wriggled a little more. 'It's just – why have you got all that old . . .' (looking for the right word, waving her hand) '. . . all that *equipment*? That stuff in your garage?'

She was talking about the fifth and last part of my Collection, of course. And if there's any one moment I can point to which marked the beginning of the events which led to the killing – quite apart from the details of my past which I've been describing, and which are more concerned with *why* rather than *when* – it was then. It accelerated the revelation of secrets, the exchange of candid information; and I should have realized from my experience with David that there are some secrets you should never tell. As my father used to say: *You live, you learn, you forget the lessons.*

Anyway, this is how I answered the question: truthfully, simply, succinctly, and with another shrug.

'It's just a hobby,' I said.

What more could I add?

This final part of my Collection is *very* specific, and is the largest of all. It consists of antique butchers' equipment manufactured by John Crampton at the end of the nineteenth century.

It all started when I stumbled across an old advertisement

for a 'Butcher Boy' Silent Electric Mincer (I still remember the catchline: *Shears the meat into strips before it reaches the knife*). I saw it in the most cherished of my five Objects – but since I promised not to discuss any more Objects until later, I won't. Nor will I be breaking that promise if I tell you that the accompanying picture inspired me. I *had* to have that mincer. And I had to have all the other equipment advertised in the Object-which-shall-remain-nameless. Nothing would stop me. *Nothing*.

Except that just about *everything* conspired to stop me. It was never going to be easy, of course, and my original aim to collect all the equipment was destined to be futile. I searched everywhere. Antiques magazines, old warehouses, butchers' shops, scrap yards, museums, attics, factories, and on and on. Some people demanded a high price, but most were happy with lies and assurances. The result is that I now own nine-tenths of what I set out to possess. Only the perishable foodstuffs are missing – and the Nopest Dusting Powder *which* KEEPS AWAY FLIES *from Hams, Bacon, Meat, etc.* I wasn't that concerned about those anyway, though the sausage casings and bindings would have been useful (and more fitting) for tonight's meal.

OK. This is how my Collection is arranged.

The smaller items are kept on shelves in the hallway. They're all made from cast iron, and include three types of mincer (the Silent Electric, the Reliance and the Large Power Model ASO), a Silent Cutter, a pie machine, a ham and gammon cutter, an electric Sausage Filler, a salting syringe, three knives, two saws, a cleaver, and a captive bolt pistol. The medium-sized items are kept on strong shelves in the garage. They are: a twenty-litre sausage filler, a portable boiler, two kinds of steam jacketted pan, three kinds of scale, a tongue-slicing machine, a fat cube and brawn-cutting machine, a bacon slicer, and a cash register. The largest items of all stand in the garage on the floor – I don't have a car – and in the shop, where they're mostly decorative. They include a smoke stove, a beef and tongue press, a sectional maple cutting block (which *still* hasn't warped or split), and a 'Butcher Boy' Cold Dry Air Refrigerator. Pride of place, however, goes to the scalding tank, a fantastic piece of equipment which can maintain an even temperature of one hundred and forty-seven degrees, and is large enough to drown a pig.

I'm sorry if you think this list over-precise. My enthusiasm for this part of my Collection isn't universally shared, and sometimes I get carried away. (Perhaps I should be carried away – old joke.)

The waiter arrived and took our order. Pizza. More bloody wheels. Kate continued from where I left her, with that worm still wriggling:

'What did your other girlfriends think about it?' she said.

'I never really had one long enough to know,' I lied. 'Anyway, that's not the point, is it? What do *you* think about it? Does it bother you?'

'No,' she said, too quickly and too lightly for it to be the whole truth. 'No – it's just that – well . . .' She waved her hands in the air. 'Ah, forget it. I'm being stupid.'

'No. Tell me.' She smiled at my bluntness, so I reinforced it with my best *you're just-being-silly* expression. It's quite a trick. You should see it.

'Well . . . it just seems a bit *odd*, that's all.' She laughed embarrassedly.

I laughed, too. A way out. 'It's less nerdy than stamps. More interesting than butterflies.'

'True.'

'Less *macabre* than stuffed animals.'

She laughed again. 'Or all those stupid gnomes in people's gardens.'

'Yeah . . .' I paused, then switched the focus. 'Haven't *you* got any weird secrets?'

'Not really,' she said, smiling.

'No books with details of secret girlie ceremonies?'

'Oh, *sure*.'

'No sticky Polaroids of self-inflicted wounds?'

'Ugh.'

'No bottles of preserved blood, or boxes of blood-stained blades from your clandestine rituals?'

'Bleah.'

'Still want your pizza?' I asked.

'I don't think I *do* anymore,' she joked. 'Do you?'

'Of course. It's time I started building up some *fat* for the winter.'

Her foot pushed against mine beneath the table, just as the meal arrived. She'd slipped off her shoes and rested the skin on her toes against a strip of my own skin, between the sock and the bottom of the trouser leg. I felt a hard-on coming on, and on it came. I couldn't help it. Nor could I help thinking about its associations.

So we come, if you'll pardon the pun, to the erect penis. The fourth of the five Symbols. The one connected with the Rite of Exposure.

You probably know by now all there is to know about the Rite of Cutting. It uses personal pain to clarify personal visions of the future, and it records that pain in a permanent form on my flesh, usually after some traumatic event. The Rite of Exposure is different: it's got nothing to do with the visions, or with pain, but is, I've since reasoned, my own way of assuaging guilt about sexual desire, and about David. (The two may not be unconnected, of course.) It began during puberty and it, too, links present and past – but in a less self-destructive and more comforting way than the Cutting. Its central element is David's dried brown Skin, which I've kept in a red, tartan-pattern shortbread tin ever since his death, and which is now, as I've said, fewer than five feet away on the shelf to my left.

This is the story. I felt in some way responsible for David's death – if not directly, then at least by association, because I should have warned him more forcefully about the thought-pictures, and stopped him cycling down that hill. I should have been more honest with him, but I wasn't, and I've lived with the . . . the self-*loathing* ever since. And I was entering puberty just as he died, too. I began to have wet dreams, which disgusted me. I saw them as an act of disloyalty, even infidelity, to David. He'd taught me the value of skin, a love for it, and all I did in return was get a hard-on for some pathetic fantasy, staining the bed like some incontinent dog. And I had to do something about it. The Rite of Cutting couldn't help, so a new Rite had to be created. The solution was obvious, now that I think about it. It's so *logical*.

This is how the ceremony ran. Any time I had an erect dick – or should I say *penis*? Some people are outraged by any word that hasn't been medically sterilized, so I'll be pleased to please them. Here goes. Any time I had an erect *penis* – whether it was after a dream, a chance encounter in the street, or just my juvenile imagination – I went up to my bedroom, locked the door behind me, and took the shortbread tin containing David's Skin from its hiding-place on the bookshelf. Then I quietly removed all my clothes, starting with my shoes and ending with my underpants, and stood naked before the small mirror in my bedroom. (I didn't have to worry about my parents listening in on me: my father was still away quite often despite his new job, and my mother respected my privacy.) Next, I positioned the mirror at an angle, so that I could see my groin when I was standing at a distance of five feet. (As I've grown up, this distance has had to be shortened – I've become quite short-sighted.) And only when I was naked, and the mirror was in the right place, did I take the Skin from the tin, raise it to my nostrils, and inhale its rich odours. This procedure went on for some time – the exact period didn't (and still doesn't) matter – but when I'd finished, I rubbed the Skin on my cheeks, across my chest, down to my stomach, on the scar on my left calf, and on my buttocks. As I did so I repeated the following words, in a cautious whisper when I was at home, but at a normal level in the private bedrooms of adulthood:

I feel the ghost of blood and bone. I feel the muscle and the flesh. Our skins are one. It is ended and begun.

Finally, I balanced that small relic of David on top of my erect penis, at the base. If my penis wasn't erect I jerked it hard until it was, always thinking about the bare, uncut flesh of his chest as I did so. And when the blood ran out of my erection, as it soon did, the ceremony was over. I put the Skin back in the tin, dressed myself, and continued as before.

But let's get one thing clear: I never masturbated to a climax during the ceremony. I'm not *sick*, for God's sake.

And another thing: David's Skin was well preserved, so don't go thinking I was waving some kind of rotten green jelly around. I'd had it sorted from the start: a few well-chosen questions in a biology lesson, and a spot of daylight robbery from the school labs, and I'd turned my prize possession into an exquisite memento, with the texture of a soft walnut and the colour of an over-ripe banana. Complete with hairs, too.

A third (and final) snippet of information for you to chew over. Today I managed to perform both a Rite of Exposure *and* a Rite of Cutting. A special day indeed.

I finished the meal in that state of tumescence, wishing I'd brought David's Skin with me. (I still feel guilty, after all these years. I've only really ever had one love, I think – and it was too pure to be sexual. It froze me in time, too. Tied me to the stake of puberty; and I've been fastened there ever since.) Anyway, if I'd brought it, I could have just nipped off to the toilet, and my anxiety, my shame, would have been assuaged immediately. But I didn't, and we're here now, and hi de ho.

At the end of it all, the waiter returned and asked if we'd like anything else. If he'd bent over any further he would have been in my lap – some people might entertain these kind of fantasies, but not me.

Kate opted for the sorbet, and I chose Death by Chocolate. This has no significance to the plot, by the way. I didn't bash someone to death with cocoa beans. I didn't stick a funnel in their mouth and choke them with hot chocolate. I didn't stab them to death with a Cadbury's Flake. It was all much less sophisticated than that.

The waiter shuffled off again, and Kate asked:

'So who's coming tomorrow?' (She was referring to the dinner party.)

'Oh, you know. The usual *boring* crowd.'

'What are you making?'

'Don't know yet. Maybe something that'll give me an excuse to use all that *weird* butchers' equipment.'

I don't like sarcasm as a rule, but it has its moments.

You may have noticed by now that we talked very little about *her*, and equally that I haven't even bothered to describe her to you. Both are entirely my fault. Narrative selection, if you like. We *did* talk a bit about her job, and what she was doing that afternoon, and what she'd be wearing to the dinner party, and how her mother was, and so on – but I don't consider these exchanges to be relevant. You might argue that after all I've been saying about giving a complete picture of the truth, I shouldn't go around wielding the editor's scissors. Maybe so. But it's my story, and you can go screw yourself.

Only kidding.

As to the second point, this is what she looks like.

She has long, black hair, thin eyebrows, a thin face with a thin nose, short, thin ears and thin lips, thin legs, a thin waist, thin arms, skinny breasts, a thin neck and thin hands (with thin fingers). She's *thin*, OK? *Not much meat on her*, as my father might have said. If you can imagine a medium-height, boyish, black-haired pipe cleaner-cum-scorzonera, you'll have her painted, framed and mounted. Some people find this sexually unappealing, but to me she is the second most beautiful person in the world. After David, obviously.

And she has that row of white scars on her left wrist, of course. Let's not forget those. Birds of a feather, and all.

'What are you thinking about?' she asked, a little later.

The desserts arrived with a double shuffle. I thanked the waiter, and he double-shuffled away. Then he double-shuffled back again, and asked (shuffling) if we wanted coffee with dessert. We did. (Shuffle, shuffle.)

'Just someone I once knew,' I told her.

'Do you want to tell me about her?' she said.

'Him.'

'Do you want to tell me about *him*, then?'

And, believe it or not, I did.

But it wasn't the whole David story. Not the visions, or the mutilation, or the cutting of his Skin; not the rabbit's foot, or the Rite of Exposure. None of the sordid stuff which is my barrier against the future, which people who can *cope* would find repellent. No: just the meat of the story. Lean reality, stripped of all trimmings. A shapeless cut of red flesh, without a hint of the animal it once was.

While I'm here, let me tell you about religion. This isn't a totally unconnected aside, honestly.

After David's accident I went through a phase of hating my thought-pictures. They were responsible for all my misery, which meant that I was responsible, too. And when you start feeling responsible for your own and others' misery, there's only one Person you can call. Jesus stood at the door, knocked, and I let him in with a guitar and a sing-a-long. I climbed a few hills, ran a few races, confessed an abridged, toned-down version of my sins before an assembled host, got fed up after a couple of weeks because the leader of the group didn't fancy me, and left. But there was one image which stayed with me: the Crucifixion. The narcissism of it. The masochism. My wounds like His. (You get something out of everything you do.)

Anyway, I'm now a committed humanist – though you wouldn't think so if you could see the state of this bathroom – and one thing I've learned is *there's no such thing as forgiveness*. You just don't get it, from yourself or from anyone else. But even if you did, I wouldn't need it. Most of the things which have happened to me have been accidental, and don't *require* absolution. I didn't intend to kill the rabbit: I only cut off its foot after it was dead, because it seemed the right thing to do, and I knew I could use it. It was the same with David: he didn't *need* his Skin – but *I* did. And if you forget about moral frameworks for a moment and consider the practical implications, it was justifiable.

And then there's tonight. You can judge for yourself when I get to that part of the story, but I don't think I really *intended* to kill. It just happened, so I had to make the best of it – and that's why I did all those apparently repellent things afterwards. When the time for my Decision comes, it, too, will be based on practical requirements, not guilt.

Back to the restaurant.

Where, when the coffee was shufflingly served, Kate took out a cigarette.

After we'd started dating, and after we both realized that we'd met before under less comfortable circumstances, at that school disco, the first thing I'd wanted to ask her was whether or not she still had the joke Lighter. Well, I got my answer at that moment. She removed it from one of her pockets, rolled the barrel, and produced another huge, flickering flame, like the one I'd seen five years before. It didn't alarm me as much, but I still winced and pulled away. She apologized with an *oops* and a *sorry* and a *clumsy me*, and then put both Lighter and cigarette on the table. She was smiling. All teeth. And, since secrets were slipping out of the bag as secrets do, she asked:

'What's the big deal with fire anyway?'

And I said, 'Why don't I tell you over dinner tonight?'

She hesitated, then grinned, then agreed – which was the main reason why, later that day, at twenty-one years of age, I lost my virginity.

11

I sometimes think I should have lost my virginity to Susan, my third friend. We've always been close in a quirky, ironic, goofy kind of way, and I've always been attracted to her . . . But, in the end, I guess I'm just not her type (let's face it – I'm not really *anyone's* type).

Whatever. It seems like a good time to tell you about Sue.

We met during the summer holidays five years ago, at a fairground. She was a juggler then. She's my oldest friend, and the second closest, if you want to be anally retentive about it. (Which I usually do, though there are times when I've taken it to extremes. At school, for example, I used to compile weekly league tables of my friends, awarding them marks out of ten for qualities such as sense of humour, how they behaved towards me, how good they were at listening, how egocentric they were, even what they looked like. Totalling the scores gave an overall tally, and thus a position. But you grow out of these things, and besides, this is supposed to be about Sue . . .) As I say, she juggles, but she's infinitely better at it than me – she's a professional children's entertainer. Two more facts. She has this way of stretching rubber bands over her face that allows her to mimic a variety of animals. And she keeps a happy box, full of cinema ticket stubs, birthday cards, locks of hair, that kind of thing. If we had nothing else in common, this desire to collect would connect us.

OK. We were spending a weekend in Cambridge. (Despite what this implies, there was, as they used to say in the seventies, *none of the other*. Sue once said that she felt like mothering me, but I laughed it off, and that was as far as it went. And we kissed too, of course – but only formally.) Anyway, she'd spent most of Saturday teaching me some advanced juggling techniques using four balls, and then we'd gone to some arty-farty cinema in the evening, and we were cycling home to her parents' house, where we were staying. The route took us along one of the paths that run away from town alongside the Cam, and there was this iron railing dividing the path from the river, to the left. It was *very* dark, I remember. Without warning, I heard a shout, then a loud clattering, followed by a stream of abuse. I stopped, turned round, and discovered that Sue had collided with one of the railings, which had broken free and was jutting into the path . . . And later that evening, she stole a traffic cone from some road works on the High Street, cycled back to the scene of the accident, and stuck it over the broken railing as a warning to others. Unlike me, she never thinks of herself. In fact—

12

Who the hell's this? I knew I should've put the answerphone on . . . Well – who knows? – it might be interesting.

Volume up, pick up the receiver . . .

'Hello.'

'Felix? Is that you?'

'Uh-huh.'

'It's me.'

'Right. Yeah . . . Dad, look, it's three o'clock in the—'

'I'm sorry to wake you—'

'You didn't. I was already up.'

'—but I've just got home. I've been on business. In Prague. I thought I'd ring and leave a message, before I came over tomorrow . . . Are you all right?'

'Yeah.'

'Good. Good. What've you been up to?'

'I had a dinner party tonight. Some friends came round – you don't know them.'

'How was it?'

'Well . . . All the food got eaten. I made some sausages, which went down well. Everyone left early, though.'

'Couldn't stand the pace, eh?'

'The toilet was blocked.'

'Right, right . . . So what've you been up to since?'

'Nothing much.'

'That's good, that's . . . Listen, Felix, I'll – do you want to talk?'

'Either way.'

'Well, look . . . It's like this. I've been speaking to a couple of people, like I said I would – you remember?'

'What are you talking about?'

'Well . . . I think I've found someone who can help you.'

'In what way, exactly?'

'OK, OK, look. Just give him a chance. I can book you in. The first consultation's free.'

'Uh-huh.'

'Yes. And it wouldn't be like what you're thinking. It's not—'

'Listen, listen—'

'Really, it's—'

'No – *Listen*. Listen to me carefully. I'm going to say this once. I'm not *ill*, I've never *been* ill, and I'm not thinking about *becoming* ill. I don't need to see a doctor, either privately or publicly, and I certainly don't need you arranging my *fucking* business for me.'

'Don't get annoyed—'

'I'm not fucking annoyed! And don't fucking patronize me!'

'Look. I'll drop the subject. It's OK. It's OK.'

'It's not OK.'

'Forget I even mentioned it, all right?'

'It's *not* OK.'

'Whatever you say, I'm sorry . . . Are you still there?'

'Yeah.'

'Do you still want me to come over tomorrow?'

'Yeah . . . Yeah, OK. Come about lunchtime.'

'Right. Good. I'll look forward to it.'

'So will I.'

'Good. Then . . . I'll be round at your place about lunchtime, OK?'

'Uh-huh.'

'Have you got any of those sausages left?'

'Nope.'

'Too bad. Well, I'll eat what there is . . . Now, you're sure you're all right?'

'*Don't* start that again—'

'No. Right. Good. So I'll see you tomorrow, Felix?'

'Hmm.'

'Goodnight.'

Prick. You're damned right you'll see me. But not *quite* in the way you – oh, hold on. I haven't turned the volume back down. My apologies. That's better. Testing, testing, one, five, eight billion.

Right. If I remember correctly, I was ready to reveal the sordid details about losing my virginity. However, since that prick who passes for my father has just seen fit to call, I'll have to postpone it.

I'm sorry: I should explain a little more. There's a single day in my past which might help you understand my feelings towards him and which, conveniently for this middle part of the narrative, fills the gap between the time David died and the time I left home.

Let's start with this:

I never really saw my mother and father for what they were. This is entirely my fault. I guess they tried to be affectionate, and treat me normally; but as far as I was concerned they were like two people at a fairground, sticking their heads through the holes of those life-size pictures of gorillas, or belly-dancers, or he-men. All mask. Two-dimensional. When you can see into the future, the people around you lose their worth.

But I'm beginning to confuse myself now. Let's start again. Start again. With the kite.

It was a huge, brightly-coloured, four-sided box kite, and it came in its own bag. The packaging said it was made from spinnaker nylon – whatever that is – held together with fibre-glass struts; all I really remember is that the box part was purple, and there were four yellow, triangular wings, and there was a hundred feet of nylon twine. When it was launched, it teased the earth by dropping and rising, over and over, but as the twine unwound it soared into the air and hung in the deep blue sky forever.

Well, you get the picture. It's a kite.

Anyway, we were on the high hill above the canal, my father and me. (Mr father was *home*, for a change. Whether he felt guilty about having missed most of my first fifteen years, I don't know; but he'd been sucked back to the nest by the vortex of my mother's illness, and he was, I suppose, just making the most of the time with me before I finally grew up. And he'd brought the kite home with him, like some crude communication tool, to try and *bond*. Pathetic, really.)

So. We were on the hill, and I said:

'How do you fly it?'

And he blustered and said something like, 'We just give it a length of twine and throw it in the air. The wind looks after the rest.'

You should know this about my father: he *was* a dragon.

This isn't just because of the nickname I gave him, and I don't mean it literally, of course. He didn't go around terrorising medieval villages, demanding sacrifices, setting knights alight, or offering to guard the golden apples in the Garden of the Hesperides (metaphorically *or* literally). He was only five feet three inches tall, he couldn't breathe fire, and he certainly couldn't fly – despite his claims to the contrary when he returned home drunk that very evening. But he was undoubtedly a *watcher*. You could tell when you talked to him that he was watching you, with unblinking eyes and smoking nostrils, from the mouth of his cave. He might pass the time of day, he might reach out a clawed hand in friendship, but come too close and his scales rose, his wings uncurled. He was a very private man, and he allowed no one to discover whether the cave he protected was filled with the world's treasures, or as empty as infinity.

But he was right about the kite; and as he walked back towards me, grinning, it soared gracefully skywards. I kept my eyes on it, releasing the twine and controlling it with a few well-timed tugs, barely noticing my father until he was standing next to me.

'It's a pity your mum's not here,' he said. 'She would have enjoyed the walk.'

*   *   *

My mother was at home, in bed. She'd been in bed for months, ever since she'd left hospital. Don't ask me to name the illness; I don't remember it. But I remember her bedroom was always dark, the curtains always drawn. She and my father were sleeping in separate rooms by then.

But this isn't – this is *not* what I want to tell you. I want to tell you that my father . . . Well, he claimed – he *claims* – she's dead. And that she died later that same day, when we went kite-flying. But I *know* he's lying. I mean – I'd spoken to her just before we left:

'Do you remember the time before I was born?' I said.

She asked me what I meant. And she *was* ill: she could barely answer.

'Before I was born,' I repeated. 'You know. *Just* before.'

She smiled. 'How can I forget? You were so heavy.'

'Did you ever talk to me?'

Her breathing was laboured; she nodded. 'A few words. Now and then.'

'*Why?*'

Her smile withered; she looked confused. 'I don't . . . I don't *understand*. Why do you keep asking these silly questions?'

I shrugged. 'I don't know.'

'You think it's *my* fault, don't you? Everything that's happened to you. You blame *me*.'

'Do you think it'll stay up?' I asked my father.

'Should do. It seems to be catching the wind all right.'

'Must be stronger up there.'

I lay down on my back holding the twine at arm's length, listening to it humming as the wind pulled it taut. I looked up at my father, leaning over me like a thick tree, and for once his eyes were heavenward, the white clouds passing over his head in a clear blue sky.

And in one of those clouds there was a vision.

What *was* the vision? It was the thing in the sink, lying in blood, blood streaks on the white enamel.

And what *is* the thing? I won't say just yet. We haven't reached that part of the story. But I'll give you a clue: it's larger than a tangerine and smaller than a buffalo.

The vision passed when my father looked down at me, but the red haze which had surrounded it was still there, and the outline of what I'd seen was superimposed on his face. This frightened me, so much so that it must have affected my expression.

'What's up?' he asked.

I said nothing, trying to remain as calm as possible; but I'd let go of the twine, and the kite spun and danced high in the air, and the wind carried it away over the field. 'Sorry,' I mumbled, 'I must've been dozing.'

'Doesn't matter,' he said. 'We can always get another one.' He almost put his arm around me, but instead he added, 'Let's go home.'

Before we do, let me tell you something else about my father.

Since I left home, about five years ago now, I've only seen him half a dozen times, though we often speak on the telephone. I haven't felt like seeing him more often; not after the mirror . . . But whatever happened to him that day, he *changed*. He was no longer the person I knew. He became an impostor.

This is why I have no regrets about leaving him this tape.

*　　*　　*

When we arrived home the house was quiet, and I rushed upstairs to my mother's bedroom. I remember my calf was hurting. I wanted to tell her about the kite, and I wanted to reassure myself she was all right. It was early evening, and the room was dark and smelled awful. Musty. Bad air. It took me a few moments to adjust after the glare of daylight, and when I did . . .

She had disappeared.

In her place, in the bed where she'd slept and suffered and stained the sheets – answering me with hoarse croaks like a big black crow – in her place was a duvet, folded roughly. I strangled a cry, ran to the window, and threw open the curtains. Low sunlight flooded in, half-blinding me, forcing me to shield my eyes and turn toward her again. My heart was beating like a tenderiser on a tough steak . . . And she *wasn't* there.

My father called me from the bottom of the stairs, and I had to force an answer:

'What?'

'Ask your mum if she wants anything from the shop.'

I left the required amount of silence, then said: 'No.'

Why didn't I tell him?

I was still sitting there when he returned. I don't know how long it was. A couple of minutes. A thousand years. Time has no meaning in such circumstances. But he must have noticed the silence as soon as he entered, because he greeted it with a loud 'Hello?' I didn't reply, and as he arrived at the foot of the stairs, bearing a bag full of shopping, he saw me. 'Felix?' he asked, though it wasn't really a question. 'Felix? What is it?'

While he was away, time had shrunk to a perpetual whirling question: *Where is she?* Now that he was back, it exploded into a rattling chain of activity. The skin of his face collapsed in despair, the shopping fell from his hands and burst like a water-bomb on the floor, and he sprinted upstairs, taking leaps of two and three steps at a time. He was past me before I could stand up, and he was by her bed as I reached the doorway.

'The phone's off the hook,' he said. I neither knew what he meant, nor how to reply. He released a low, despairing wail like a sick animal, a noise I'd never heard from him, or anyone else, before.

And I had a sudden, vivid recollection, a regurgitation, of the vision I'd seen many years earlier. The one which showed my father straightening his jacket in front of the mirror in our hallway; then disappearing and returning, dressed differently. Using a piece of chalk and a pogo stick, if you recall, I'd taken this to mean an impostor would arrive in our house. So I said nothing. The time had almost come, and I needed to be prepared.

He turned around. His face was swollen with unbroken tears. He opened his mouth, but nothing came out, not even that inhuman wail. Then he stood up – his clothes were dishevelled from kneeling by the bed – and he wiped the tears from his eyes, and moved towards me. Briefly, I thought he was going to hold me, to reassure us both that everything would be fine; but he brushed past me as if I wasn't there and vanished into the bathroom. Now you see him, now you don't. I looked at the empty space in the bed, and that nagging question whirled within me.

My father emerged from the bathroom dry-eyed and red-faced, his clothes still untidy. This time he *did* notice me.

'Will you be all right?' he asked.

I didn't really understand what he meant, so I said: 'I think so.'

'I'm going out,' he announced abruptly. 'Only for a couple of hours. I think she must have called them. She said if things got bad . . .' He stopped. 'Well, I'll be back soon.' He looked away and descended the stairs quickly. I stood at the top of the landing, watching him as he turned towards the mirror. He straightened his trousers first, pulling the knees down and flattening out the creases. Then he tugged at his shirt, tucked it into his trousers, and repositioned his tie. Finally, he straightened his jacket, smoothing out the pockets against his hips. 'You're sure you'll be all right?' he repeated.

I told him I'd be fine.

I looked at the open door of my mother's bedroom. Pale light filtered through it onto the landing. And when I turned back again, my father had gone. I hadn't heard the front door open or close, and at first I thought he might still be in the hallway; but I checked the downstairs rooms, then upstairs, and he wasn't there. Now you see him, now you don't. It was puzzling, but it convinced me of the truth of my vision. My real father was gone forever, and the impostor was about to make his appearance. Devil or daddy – all I had to do was sit and wait.

And I waited for five hours, until the whole house was dark; until I fell asleep. I told you earlier how I believe that my father was sucked in by the mirror in the hallway. I imagine it reaching out with fine, spun threads of glass, wrapping around him, penetrating his flesh, piercing and teasing him, wrenching him inside the frame. Well . . . after five hours, he returned from that ordeal.

Did he suffer any pain along the way? I don't know. But I hope so.

No journey should be without pain.

*   *   *

I've never been able to escape from mirrors. They're every-where I look. My mother and father were mirrors; my girl-friend's eyes are mirrors; my friends are mirrors. Everyone, if you can ignore that immediate illusion of depth, is a polished, two-dimensional, infinitely thin pane of glass; and if you could see round the back of them, all you'd find is shining silver. But you can't. The glass is always pointed towards you, and all you see is yourself.

Look at me. Can't you see the deep wounds lining your own face after the Cutting? Can't you see that loose, dead skin hanging from your own body; the streaks of blood, the net-work of scars? Can't you see the two of us, hand in hand, lying in this bath?

Anyway, I woke when I heard shuffling in the hallway. Un-steady feet, a loud crash, a curse. The light was switched on, then off again almost immediately. I stood up slowly. The light came on again. A bear-like man stood at the foot of the stairs, preceded by his thick shadow. He was bent almost double, supporting himself with a stubby hand on the second step. He looked ready to vomit. His face was red and swollen; monster-like. And he was very, very drunk.

The impostor had arrived.

Did the mirror in the hallway shimmer in appreciation of its child, as he doubled up next to it? Of course it didn't. As I've already told you, mirrors are far too clever for that. They're as casual as clams when you're watching, but take your eyes off for just one second and they'll suck you in before you can say – well, *anything*. Doppelganger, for example.

He called my name as he climbed the stairs. I backed away. 'It's only me,' he said. He tried to sound in control, but when he opened his mouth the soul of a crate of beer escaped.

'What's up? Don't you recognize me?' I retreated further, avoiding my mother's room, aiming vaguely for my own. 'Don't you recognize me?' he repeated, following me, grabbing my arm.

I asked him to let me go, but the words uncorked his anger.

'Let you go? I'll bloody let you go . . . First *she* leaves me, now you want to bloody go, too . . . Well then, go ahead. Run.' I broke free and rushed for the bedroom door. 'Run *fucking* run rabbit run!' Before I could close it behind me his foot was jammed into the gap. 'Let me in,' he said pathetically.

I wouldn't.

'Let me in or I'll give you such a damn pasting you won't sit down for a fucking year!'

I pulled away as he pushed the door inwards. He didn't frighten me – in fact, I felt sorry for him. He was a feeble impostor, and neither his aggression nor his sympathy could provoke me. But I couldn't have anticipated his next move. He walked to the window overlooking the back garden, and said, simply:

'I can fly.'

I didn't know what to say.

'I can,' he insisted. 'All I have to do is uncurl these wings, open the window and leap out. Leap high. And I'll fly so high you won't see me again for a month.' He laughed.

'You're drunk,' I told him. 'You should go to bed.' (Even impostors need a little sympathetic advice now and then.)

'I have something to tell you first,' he said; and I expected him to confess the whole business about the mirror. But he didn't. 'It's important, so listen carefully. I want you to listen. Carefully . . . Your mother wanted you. She did. But I didn't care either way. So listen. You're no son of mine. I never wanted you, and I won't have anything more to do with you.'

And he slapped me hard across the cheek.

In the morning, as we cleaned up the house, he apologized for everything he'd said; but it was too late.

The damage was done.

Back to the night before.

He closed the door behind him, and I was in a dark room with a stinging cheek and a whistling echo in my ear. I was in a house of strangers and shadows, with no one to rely on but myself.

One logical course immediately suggested itself. I sneaked out onto the landing. It was quiet, empty, but there was a light on downstairs. I crept into the bathroom and switched on the light, closing and locking the door; then I stripped off and sat down on the side of the bath. I took my father's five-pack of razor blades, selected one, unwrapped the paper, and made an incision with the blade on the top of my right thigh. I began with the rectangular mirror frame, then carved a representational image of my father's face staring from it. Behind his head, if you look closely enough, you can see a blood-red box-kite caught on the breeze. (This is now a faint, white scar which has almost disappeared. A pity.) It was easy work; and when it was over, I began carving an image of the blade itself on the opposite thigh. This is the fifth and final Symbol, and it epitomizes all the blades and other cutting tools I've used over the years.

I stood up, letting the blood run down my thighs, and looked in the mirror, the one which now hangs here in my own bathroom. It wasn't large enough to pull me through to its own world, so I wasn't afraid of it. I put my face almost flat against the glass, trying to peer through to the other side – but there was nothing. This angered me, and for a moment I lost control, giving the glass a half-hearted head-butt. There was a quick crunching sound, and when I pulled my head away there was a hairline crack in the reflection, running from the bottom left corner to the middle of the right hand side. This gave me an inexplicable feeling of great power; so much so that I burst out laughing.

And then I broke every mirror in the house.

13

OK. Just to keep you up-to-date:

What you know: all of the Symbols, all of the Collection, and two of the Objects. If I now mention blades, or rabbit's feet, or flames, or bicycles, or penises, or scalpels, or skin, or stored remnants of Rites of Cutting, or antique butcher's equipment, I hope you'll understand their special Significance for me. (Whether or not you care is up to you.)

What you don't know: the final three Objects, the thing floating in the sink, how I fell in love with Kate, and what happened between yesterday afternoon and the moment I switched on this cassette recorder.

I'll begin with yesterday afternoon and lead you through the last five years in the same breath. It's an abrupt leap, I know, and I make no apologies; but the truth is, there isn't much to tell. Odd children don't always grow up to become odd adults. In fact, until tonight, I thought I was going to get out of jail free, and lead a mundane life spiced with the odd dash of self-mutilation. And who would have cared? What goes on behind closed doors is a person's own business; and with me, the doors are firmly closed. I certainly didn't whip out the Skin at parties, and no one – but no one – saw *all* the scars until today.

After the bill had been paid – this is yesterday afternoon again, at the restaurant – the waiter shuffled away, and Kate and I descended the spiral stairs to the street. And we held hands for a while, and made jokes, and confirmed the arrangements for that evening, and kissed, and parted.

I went back to work – and before we go any further, I should tell you more about what I do (and have done for the past three years).

I'm a junior partner in a butcher's shop. It's no *ordinary* butcher's – or so we like to think. There's a hint of upmarket, 'traditional' meat stall about it, a few touches of delicatessen, and only the merest sniff of the abattoir thrown in. There's not even a fragment of a memory of an echo of supermarket, or vacuum-wrap, or pre-packaged goods. Three of us work there full-time: myself, my business partner and friend, John, and an apprentice, whose name I'm always getting wrong even though he's been with us for over a year. It's either Denzil or Darren, and if I searched through the other tape I'd remember, because John and I discussed him on the phone earlier. Anyway, long story short, whenever I walk into the shop (which I invite you to imagine me doing right now), I just say *hello* or *good morning*. It saves a lot of trouble.

The shop in general. We sell everything that makes

meat-eaters' mouths water, that flesh-eaters fight for, the chow that carnivores crave, the belly timber that builds the best, the tucker that tickles the tum – well, you soon discover the limits of advertising jargon.

The shop in detail. We sell salted beef, beef flatribs, beef joints, venison steaks, venison sausages, venison (diced), quails' eggs, Scotch eggs, free range hens' eggs, calves' hearts, lambs' brains, pigs' livers, pigs' kidneys, pigs' trotters, tripe, haggis, faggots, black pudding, veal cutlets, streaky bacon, lean bacon, bacon joints, gammon hocks, picnic hams, turkeys, rabbits, pigeons, quails, all kinds of offal, all sorts of sausages, all types of pie. It's a world of blood-red, brown, yellow and pink-white meat, thick white fat tied with string, corn-coloured chicken, milk-white veal, ivory bones. A collage of speckles and ribs, streaks and smoke lines, mottles and ridges.

I know it off by heart.

So, after lunch I walked in through the open glass doors and inhaled those wonderful, thick, rich odours of fresh meat. (I always do. It's a tradition.) I shouted a cheery *good afternoon*, and went to change my clothes. I was in a great mood.

When I came out, John was standing by the table – I'm talking the thick, heavy, iron-bound variety – and he was chopping something which looked suspiciously like horse meat. His apron was smeared with dried blood. And the apprentice was staring at me as if I should remember his name, so I ignored him, and he stared instead through the window at the café opposite. This café is the kind of place where, if you run your hands under the chair frames, you're liable to find your fingers covered in odd blobs of slime and curly black hairs.

'What do you want me to do?' I asked John.

He didn't look up from the horse meat. 'There's some

chitterlings want cleaning. Or we've got some cow's heels. You could boil them up, strip them . . . It's up to you.'

'Since when have we sold cow heels?'

He tutted. 'We *don't* sell them. I was *joking*.'

John has a sense of humour so dry I often don't find him funny at all. When I rang him on Thursday to invite him to the dinner party, his reply was *no*. He threw the phone down, and rang me back immediately to say *yes*. Then he hung up again, and rang back again, and said: 'Ask me tomorrow.'

'Great joke,' I told him. He was carving some intricate pattern in the horse; I didn't want to ask why. 'Are you still coming to the dinner party?'

'If you're cooking.'

'I am.'

'Then I am.'

'So what *does* need doing?' I persisted.

'Dog biscuits,' he said.

'Dog biscuits?'

'Dog biscuits.'

'Is there an echo in the room?'

'Is there an echo in the room?'

I gave him a withering look, but he had his hand up the horse's ass.

This is the recipe for dog biscuits. Dog biscuits are handy because they use up all the odds and ends of meat, scraps and scrags of beef, hog livers, hog rings – generally, the kind of food we can't normally sell. The rinds are especially important, because they bind the whole thing together. Anyway, you stick the ingredients in a cooking kettle, and boil them in just enough water to cover them. Once the whole lot is cooked, you save the liquid, remove the meat, grind it through a mincer, and stick the mince back in the kettle. Throw in some maize meal until you get a stiff paste, and then cook the lot for another twenty minutes, stirring all the time. Finally, you empty the kettle, shape the paste into bones, or fish, or llamas, or whatever the hell you like, and leave them to dry.

This took me just over an hour; and I spent the time remembering all the other jobs I had before this one. This is a summary of those thoughts (which, incidentally, fill in the first two years between leaving home and today).

Job One: The Wages Clerk. This was my first employment after I left school, and it was intended as a tribute to my father. (Not the impostor. *He* wanted me to go to university; but that's another story, and I won't bother you with it.) It lasted about nine months, and introduced me to the cut-throat jungle of accounts, spreadsheets, adding machines, timed tea breaks, computer print-out mountains, and disgruntled employees spitting fire whenever their pay packets went a penny short. It was a savage, dog-eat-dog-then-dog-look-for-another-dog-to-eat-because-it's-still-hungry world, where mild-mannered heroes fought tedious monetary minotaurs in the dull labyrinths of company fiscal policy . . . (Well, *that* was a bit florid, wasn't it? Unlike the job.) In the end all those numbers bored me fucking stiff, so I took an extended unofficial holiday halfway through, and found myself in . . .

Job Two: The Fairground Assistant. This was pretty boring manual work – a summer job which only lasted three months – but it's how I met Sue. She spent ten weeks teaching me various juggling techniques, and I only mention it now to show that I know what I'm talking about when, later on, I use the hackneyed metaphor about writing being just like juggling (pin back your lugholes for Job Four in a couple of minutes).

Thanks to Sue's tuition, I worked *magic* with four balls: heading them, kicking them, bouncing them on the ground, catching them behind my back, balancing them on my chin, spinning them, throwing them against walls, and (as a finale) tossing them high in the air and letting them fall into four different pockets . . . Well, on a *good* day, at any rate. (By the way, I did not, as you may have been led to believe by the earlier part of this narrative, carry out my threat to juggle pigs' kidneys yesterday afternoon. The shop was too busy, and though I'm a hedonist first and a meat technician second, I didn't think this would create the appropriate image for a family butcher. Perhaps I'm wrong. Perhaps it's precisely the route we should be taking). Right:

JOB THREE: The Butcher's Apprentice. I spent just under a year learning the trade, before establishing my own business with the help of John's cash. *Establishing* is the wrong word: *leeching* on his cash and experience is nearer the mark. Our previous employer was a greasy, hairy, middle-aged, monosyllabic man built like a mastodon. What he did with dead animals should have resulted in life imprisonment. If there was a National Association for the Protection of Animals, Livestock and Meat, he would have been locked up. *Abuse* is an inadequate word. And I don't want to talk about him any more, so:

JOB FOUR: The Door-to-Door Axe Murderer. This one's a joke. If your sides are splitting, call an ambulance. If not, I'll try again:

JOB FOUR: The Writer. *How could you be a writer at the same time as you were a butcher?* you may ask. And I may answer: *It's none of your business.* Actually, there's no big secret. They happened at the same time.

*   *   *

Here's another brief aside. Indulge me, if you will, while I discuss that old, old cliché: *Writing is just like juggling*.

Well, it is, and it isn't.

It is: You toss all your ideas, and characters, and plots into the air, watch them rise and fall, and interact, and spin around, and then you have to catch them all again. If you fail to hold on to just one, your audience will spot the mistake, and your performance will be ruined . . . Something else, too. You have to vary your routine or it becomes repetitive and mundane . . . And both disciplines involve hands (unless you're dictating) . . . And that's about all I can think of.

OK. *It isn't*: Writing and juggling are two very different things. You don't need coloured balls filled with sand or foam or beans when you're writing, and few jugglers have ever juggled with a pen, a typewriter, or even a cassette recorder – and certainly not with five hundred sheets of A4 paper.

Anyway, the truth is, I was never very good at juggling *or* writing. The balls got dropped. The stories were never finished.

This one is no different.

'Why are you grinning like an idiot?' John asked.

'Just thinking,' I told him.

'Makes a change,' I heard the apprentice mumble (he's a great friend both to the cliché and the Book of Old Jokes).

'Have you cleaned the freezer yet?' I asked him.

He murmured something and shook his head slowly, like some deranged animal in a zoo.

'Why don't you, then?' I suggested.

He disappeared into the freezer, sulking. (He was eighteen last week.)

'What were you thinking *about*?' John persisted.

I told him I'd been remembering all the jobs I'd done before this one.

'Felix Fly, Crap Writer . . .' he offered.

'And the wages clerk. And the fairground where I learned to juggle.'

'I didn't know you could juggle.'

'You never asked.'

'*Touchy.*'

I changed the subject. 'What can I make tomorrow night?'

'For the dinner?'

'Yeah.'

'Meat.' He nodded; pleased with his laconicism.

'How about sausages?'

'Sausages?'

'Sausages.'

He smiled. 'Sausages is fine by me.'

I switched direction again. 'Who's on serving this afternoon?'

'I am.'

'Well, look over there. We've got customers waiting.'

He peered around the partition that separates the meat preparation area from the serving counter, and saw a queue of five people, most of them annoyed. Despite his limp – a legacy of his cycling accident – he glided like an ice-skater over the polished floor, and was serving quicker than you can say *home-rendered lard*.

I shouted for Denzil to bring me a pig from the cold store. He did, eventually, and I set to work on the head, starting with a small cut about an inch behind the ears. I found the joint, gave the ear a sharp pull and a twist, and cut away the rest of the head with a knife. This description is, of course, an artificial device which allows me to tell you what's happened to

which looks more like a butterfly, or a fancy dress mask, than twin loops. It's in reasonable condition, though.

RIGHT CALF: One bicycle, each wheel with thirteen spokes. Very pale.

LEFT THIGH (FRONT): A razor blade, approximately five times normal size, with drops of blood falling from it towards the inside of my thigh. I regret the blood now: it's in poor taste and somewhat clichéd. Both blade and blood are perfectly visible.

LEFT THIGH (REAR): An extensive tessellation of hexagons and triangles, created for no other reason than the fact that I was *extremely* bored one afternoon a couple of years ago. It's probably the most accurate, satisfying and well-defined carving on my entire body.

RIGHT THIGH (FRONT): A mirror, reflecting my real father's face and the (now faint) kite.

RIGHT THIGH (REAR): A set of four juggling balls being tossed into the air by a pair of disembodied hands. Easily discernible; though, of course, it can't capture the colour and life of the originals.

LEFT BUTTOCK: A rather striking copy of Harborth's tiling, which resembles a sunflower, or an exploding firework, but lacks the precise detail of the original. For me, it epitomizes a short, high-pitched fart; hence its location. It's still quite pink.

RIGHT BUTTOCK: Escher's 1960 woodcut, Circle Limit IV. Unfinished. Poor quality. It's impossible to distinguish the devils from the angels.

PENIS: No comment.

STOMACH: A pentagon of sausages arranged around the navel. Fresh and scabbed.

LOWER CHEST: A collection of geometric solids. This is a linked, semicircular sequence which runs from one armpit to the other, below the nipples, and incorporates a truncated dodecahedron, a small rhombicosidodecahedron, a rhombicuboctahedron, a quintet of five-pointed stars, and five pentagons. The three-dimensional shapes are now virtually unrecognizable. The flat shapes are still clear.

UPPER CHEST: A large, distinct, reversible head which, depending on the way it's viewed, represents God or the Devil. From my point of view, looking down, it's the Devil. No symbolism is intended. I'm proud of the way it's turned out; though, naturally, it prevents me wearing V-neck jumpers without a shirt.

BACK: Crude copies of Escher designs, including the 1952 wood-engraving, Dragon, (eating its own tail), and four of the imaginary creatures from the 1951 lithograph, Curl-Up (these resemble articulated lizards with square, bony heads and bulbous black eyes). I'm particularly proud of my interpretation of Escher's 1948 lithograph, Drawing Hands, in which each hand appears to be holding a scalpel and carving my skin. Surrounding this trio is a collection of household utensils, including four knives, two tin-openers, a spatula, a large spoon and two three-pronged forks. All would be barely recognizable to anyone else but me.

LEFT UPPER ARM: Flames. Still animated, but faded.

RIGHT UPPER ARM: Five of the flatworms from Escher's 1959 lithograph, Flat Worms. All very clear.

LEFT AND RIGHT FOREARMS: Nothing.

HANDS: No comment.

NECK: Nothing. This isn't simply for cosmetic reasons: I've

just never had the confidence to carve anywhere near the jugular.

FACE: No comment.

HEAD: A straight line, running from the nape of my neck to the top of my forehead. It was cut with the aid of the blade from a pencil sharpener, and two mirrors. It's only been seen in its entirety by my hairdresser, and is a ridged wound, quality unknown.

Where I've offered no comment in this list, I'll reveal the details towards the end of the story, because they're all part of the Rites of Cutting performed this afternoon and evening. And if you're wondering about all the Escher designs, I can only say that there's no Significance attached to them beyond my own admiration for the artist.

I'd almost finished carving the pig when John appeared.

'Haven't you finished carving that pig yet?' he said.

'Does a bear shit in a public lavatory?' I quipped.

'It does if it comes to my town,' he countered.

So far, I'd followed routine with the pig: first, you split the cerebral column; then you cut off the fore end between the fourth and fifth ribs, cut the leg off a couple of inches below the pelvic bone, saw through the ribs to remove the loin, and divide the forequarters by sawing through the ribs and blade bone. All I had to do was slice through the forelegs close to the breast, and it was over.

'About time, too,' John said.

'Is there no one waiting to be served?' I suggested.

'If there was, I'd be serving, wouldn't I?'

'Would you?'

'I would.'

I checked the serving counter. It was late afternoon and the shop was deserted. Only the quiet hum of the refrigerator disturbed the peace. It was almost time to prepare the ingredients for the dinner party.

I wouldn't like you to get the wrong impression about the relationship between John and me. There's absolutely no hostility. He's probably my closest friend since David, and if I was going to reveal my scars to anyone last night, it should have been him. But he's never seen them, and doesn't even know they exist. Apart from his cycling accident, the other main reason I like him is because he tried to kill himself, a fact which immediately made him interesting. I admired him, too – because he shared the knowledge with me almost as soon as I met him.

When he was thirteen, he wrote a book of poems, hailed by his school-friends as a seminal work, the essence of true poetry, a distillation of the love, hate, fear and ecstasy of Everyman; and so on. He sent it off to a wide range of poetry magazines and publishers, expecting fame and international recognition within six months at the outside . . . And, of course, all the manuscripts boomeranged back by return of post, together with photocopied rejection slips. The comments ranged from *Thank you for sending us your poetry, but . . .* to *juvenile claptrap*; encompassing *we haven't the space, please subscribe to our magazine*, and *it's not our kind of thing* along the way. John says he tried to commit suicide at the time, but now, looking back on his poetry, he realizes why it was rejected. *Pretentious, florid shite*, he calls it. But I've read it, and I think he's too harsh.

Since he told me all this, I've thought about suicide on and off. About the methods, and the tools, and the notes. The notes, in particular, always sound fine when you're depressed, but melodramatic and foolish the next morning. This is one reason why I haven't committed myself so far. Another is that I can't decide on the best method. Jumping off a bridge takes guts – and it's inconvenient for the people who scrape you up or fish you out. Hanging might give you nothing more than a nasty rope burn if you get the knot wrong. Swallowing pills takes ages, and there's always the threat of the dreaded stomach pump. Shooting yourself in the head might leave you a vegetable.

In fact, the best compromise I've come up with is a sliding scale of incisions, gauged according to the level of desire to self-destruct. It works as follows:

A TINY INCISION for bad news, such as your football team being relegated, or an unsolvable problem that just won't go away.

A SMALL INCISION for slightly worse news or occurrences, such as the death of a favourite plant, or a distant aunt.

A MEDIUM INCISION for a Rite of Cutting, or an act of masochistic self-mutilation, or a release. I've lived in this band for most of my life.

A LARGE INCISION for moods induced by acts of such depravity or perversity that I couldn't possibly describe them here.

A FATAL INCISION for unforgivable acts. Murder, for example. Or lying. Or cheating at chess. And so on.

Let me make this clear. I'm not *recommending* this line of behaviour. That wouldn't be responsible of me, would it? All I'm saying is, if you're anything like me, it's a useful reference tool which lets you do the job with a minimum of fuss. In fact, I've even tried refining it even further by introducing factors which affect the length and depth of a cut, such as the level of guilt, or pain, or time – but this simple reckoner is still the most effective. It means you can avoid committing suicide when, deep down, you don't really want to do it; but you still have a permanent reminder that a Bad Thing has happened, or is happening, to you.

You could, of course, pull yourself together. But it's much easier tearing yourself apart.

'I'll see you tomorrow night,' was the last thing I said to John yesterday afternoon.

'Unless you lock yourself in the freezer over the weekend,' he replied.

Darren tried to slip out of the door without saying anything, so I said *goodnight* pointedly. He sniggered, mumbled unintelligibly, sniggered again, and left. I cleaned off the chopping board, wiped down the glass on the display counter and locked the cold store. Then I took out the ingredients and ready-made snacks for the dinner party, wrapped them in plastic bags (one of our *few* concessions to modern technology), bundled up half a dozen sausage skins, grabbed hold of a clean saw, a carving knife, and a cleaver, and turned out the lights. Finally, I locked the door behind me and headed for home.

Which is where I'd continue this narrative . . . But I need a break, so I'll tell you about Alison instead.

14

Alison is the only other person I know who's as obsessive as I am. The difference is, her obsession is cars.

Alison *loves* cars. Fast ones. The faster the better. What she's really looking for is a Lamborghini that can travel faster than light, but she works in the marketing department of a small, unknown publishing house, and they don't pay her that kind of money. But she has dreams. She wants to be *large*. And *famous*. Like most car freaks, she's addicted to jargon, too. She says *sparks* when she means spark plugs; and she substitutes *distrib* for distributor, *hammer* for accelerator, *dash* for dashboard, *stick* for gear lever, *carb* for carburettor, *anchors* for brakes, and on and on. It never ends. I asked her once if she called the wheels *whees*, or the steering wheel a *st*, but she didn't find it funny. It *isn't* funny, I admit – but what *is* absolutely hilarious is that she keeps a shotgun and five hundred cartridges in her car boot. I only found out why this evening . . . A few more facts. We met two years ago. She's a regular customer, and it was John who got to know her first, and she's been trying to get him up against the freezer door ever since. She's also a distant friend of Kate's, though the link is too convoluted to explain, and involves all sorts of shared childhood memories. Oh – and she lives alone in a second-floor flat in the centre of town.

One lunchtime, about a year ago, she was cycling into town from work. She wanted to buy the latest Philip's road atlas (she laughed bitterly at this point in the story, though I've no idea why), and it was a windy day. And she was approaching a junction where two roads meet in a sort of Y-shape, and there are cars approaching from both sides. And, as she was drifting left to meet the traffic, her rear wheel hit the kerb and buckled. Simple as that. *The rim*, she explained. *Stress fracture . . . hairline crack . . . metal fatigue.* Anyway, she fell arse-over-tit and ended up with a bruised knee and an impressive friction burn up her thigh, which she's since revealed to John on several occasions . . . But, I have to tell you, I don't quite believe her story. What actually happened, I suggest, was that she fell off her bike because she was simply too eager to get to that road atlas. She just wasn't *concentrating*. These things happen.

15

OK, I'm ready now. Let's talk about love.

It's yesterday. It's my house. It's seven p.m.

I opened the front door.

I'd already cooked most of the dinner, but the main course – osso buco – was giving me a headache. If you don't know anything about it, this is what it involves: sealing the meat in hot oil with a coating of flour, frying some onion and garlic, deglazing the pan with about half a pint of wine, and stirring in some stock, tomatoes and bouquet garni. Simple. But the simmering is always the most worrying time: as the sauce reduces, you've got to keep your eye on the pan to check it hasn't dried out, adding more liquid if it needs it. It means, basically, that you can never fully commit yourself to a conversation. And tonight, of all nights, I wanted to talk.

So there was Kate, standing on the threshold, grinning. Her summer coat was damp, and there was a fine drizzle illuminated by the street light behind her.

'It's me,' she said.

'I can see,' I said. 'Come in.'

She sniffed the air like a weasel. 'Something smells nice.'

I told her it probably wasn't the food.

I like a joke, now and then.

Kate's full name is Katharine Lord. When I first met her, and remembered who she was, and suffered a few unanticipated thought-pictures in the process (and bad ones at that) – when I first met her, I looked for *meaning* in that name. The naming dictionary told me it meant *pure*; but even now I can't see how purity fits the pattern of what happened. It's just another dead end. Sometimes you can search for Significance until your head falls off, but it isn't always there to be found. If she'd been called Felicity, there would have been no escaping it.

Things hardly ever work out in the way you expect.

I took her coat, and led her through to the living room (the second door on the right), past the shelves holding the three mincers, the Silent Cutter, the pie machine, the ham and gammon cutter, the electric Sausage Filler, the salting syringe, the captive bolt pistol, three knives, two saws, and a cleaver.

I suggested she put some music on.

'Any requests?' she said.

I couldn't decide. 'You choose . . . I'll just put this away.'

I carried her coat into the bedroom. It was warm on the inside, cold on the outside. I draped it over the bed, and it lay there like a wet, white seal skin. I didn't mind the dampness on the bedclothes; in fact, if I'm honest, I *liked* it. When I returned, there was a shrill tune piping from the speakers, which I didn't recognize.

'It's the radio,' she explained, noticing my puzzled expression.

She was kneeling on the floor, skimming through an old book of mine. I couldn't see the title, but something about it made me uneasy.

'Do you want a drink?' I offered. 'I've got water, orange juice, beer—'

'Wine?'

'Of *course*. Red or white?'

She opted for red – the most suitable accompaniment for the dinner I'd planned anyway – and I went to the kitchen and filled two glasses to the brim: hers first, then my own. I had to bend down and suck off the excess.

As I handed her the wine, she looked up, and thanked me, and turned the page absent-mindedly. I glanced down and realized why I'd felt so uneasy about the book. It was my volume of Escher prints, and it was open at Circle Limit IV, and there was a thick line of dried brown blood, about three inches long, slicing the page in two, cutting through a group of black devils and white angels . . . I was *horrified*. I hadn't looked at it for over two years, and I must have forgotten to clean up after the last Cutting. I could still see myself, looking at the print, then at my buttock reflected in a mirror, trying to copy the pattern on my skin with the Scalpel, spots of blood dripping onto the paper. The image was so ridiculous, so out of place amongst all this normality, that I laughed out loud.

'What's so funny?' she asked, looking down. Then she saw it. 'Ugh! What *is* that?'

'Gravy,' I laughed. 'I remember spilling it. I was reading and eating my dinner on the sofa, and . . . What a *pillock*.' I pulled my face into a dunce mask. She examined the stain, sniffed it, scraped away at the crusty surface with her fingernail, and grimaced. 'I should have wiped it up. It's probably infested with all kinds of mutant bacteria now. You'll end up with two heads.'

'Two heads are better than one,' she quipped – rather weakly I thought. But the danger had passed. She turned the page, flicking the dried blood from her finger, and then put down the book. 'So when are you going to show me that stuff in the garage?'

'Whenever,' I said.

'Can I have a look now?'

"Course you can . . . I'll just turn down the main course.'

'Uh-huh. What is it?'

'That'd be *telling*.'

Her bluntness, her inquisitiveness – it was all a test. I knew that. She was prodding me, poking the animal, seeing how it reacted. Was it tame? Could she make friends with it? Could she make *love* to it? Or was it just too *weird*? And I'm so tempted to fail. So tempted to give her those four boxes on the high shelf in the garage, to answer all her questions. I can see her now. She opens the first box and finds all the used Scalpel blades; opens the next and discovers the Polaroids, each one showing a new patch of wounded skin; opens the third and finds bottles and cans and jam jars and sealed tumblers of blood; opens the fourth, the biggest of them all, and tips out fifteen diaries. And when she opens the diaries, she reads the account of every Cutting, and she notices the brown stains, and she makes the connection. And what then?

'I'll just get the key,' I told her. (I keep the door to the garage locked as a precaution.) I went back into the kitchen and turned down the gas beneath the osso buco – not a moment too soon, either. Then I grabbed the key: I keep it on a hook, at eye level, just beneath the shortbread tin, which is on the shelf above the fridge. These details are important.

'How come you keep it locked?' Kate asked, putting her arms around my waist. She'd sneaked up on me, and I froze briefly, then forced myself to relax.

'I've got some valuable stuff in there,' I said. 'Well, it's valuable to *me* . . .'

'Uh-huh.' She stroked my head.

'. . . but I don't think any of it's worth more than a few quid – if that.'

'Right.' She kissed the back of my neck, and I turned around and . . . Well, things got pretty boring for about fifteen minutes.

At the end of it, I had to add some more water to the osso buco. Then I turned the key in the lock and pushed the garage door open, holding it ajar with my foot, against the tension of the spring.

'Actually,' I said, wearing my best guilty expression. 'I've got something to confess . . . This is where I keep my collection of frozen animal heads.'

'Oh, *very* amusing,' she said wearily.

She slipped past me, and led me in with her hand. The door closed behind us with a sharp click. For a moment we were in semi-darkness: I could see Kate, a silhouette standing absolutely still, waiting for me to turn on the light. I groped for the switch on the wall behind the door, and found it; but I paused, watching her grainy, grey, two-dimensional outline.

the Rite of Cutting and the Rite of Exposure in the past five years. So here we go:

The need for both Rites has declined since I left home, though for different reasons. The Rite of Exposure continues to serve as an antidote to sexual desire, though less obsessively; and you can assume that for every girlfriend I've had in the past five years (and there are few enough to detail all of them soon), there's been a corresponding Rite of Exposure. It's more of a symbolic gesture now, with a single ceremony covering all instances of sexual desire in any particular relationship. The Rite of Cutting has drifted even further from its origins. Since I left home, the thought-pictures have become less frequent, and the Rite has become more of a hobby than a need. But I get too much pleasure from self-mutilation to surrender it altogether.

Today was slightly different, of course. I performed a rather special Cutting ceremony, which involved facial *and* bodily mutilation. My excuse is: it was a triumphant farewell to the Rite. There'll be no more. And since there *won't* be another, here's an exhaustive catalogue of the shape and condition of every Cutting I've performed to date, from head to toe. Some are a response to visions, or to Significant events; others are there just for their own sake.

Whatever:

LEFT FOOT: A rabbit's foot. Crude and faint.

RIGHT FOOT: An image of my own head, as seen in a mirror. Not a brilliant likeness – the hair's all wrong – but still quite recognizable.

LEFT SHIN, RIGHT SHIN: Nothing.

LEFT CALF: A crap representation of the Lorenz attractor,

The room was quiet, and cold, and smelled of dust . . . And I switched on the light. Gas buzzed and flickered in the fluorescent tube, then burst into white fire, igniting the whole room. She squinted, flinched, then surveyed her surroundings. Two long white walls, one completely bare, one broken by wide wooden shelves; a short wall with a black door, against which I was leaning. An up-and-over garage door, permanently locked. A white ceiling. A grey concrete floor . . . She'd been here before, of course. But only briefly. And only as part of an introductory tour. She hadn't asked any questions then, but she must have been thinking about it since.

She turned first towards the large equipment, on the floor: the beef and tongue press, the Cold Dry Air Refrigerator, the scalding tank. She peered over the sides of the tank, saw that it was dry and uninteresting. (It *is* pretty dull when it's not being used.) Her gaze turned upwards towards the shelves, towards the sausage filler, the portable boiler, the steam jacketted pans, the scales, the tongue-slicing machine, the fat cube and brawn-cutting machine, the bacon slicer, the cash till. The tiny muscles around her mouth and eyes registered no reaction. On the far right of the top shelf she saw four plain, cardboard boxes.

'What's in those?' she asked.

And I told the truth. 'Oh, you know . . . Used *Scalpel* blades, pictures of *wounds*, bottles of *blood*, records of masochistic *rituals*. The usual.'

She barked a sarcastic laugh. 'Har *har* . . . Is it more of this stuff?' She indicated the rest of the Collection.

What could I say? I'd hoped she'd swallow the wisecrack. I couldn't *repeat* the joke, because there was a slim chance it might backfire. And I'd made it twice today already . . . So I said:

'Just some bits and pieces. Hooks, knives, that kind of thing.'

'Ooh – let's have a look.' Her enthusiasm surprised me, and I hesitated, so she pressed: 'I'm interested. *Really*.'

And I grumbled, and mumbled, and said it was all pretty boring stuff, and I didn't want her to think I was *weird*, and I was embarrassed about showing her anyway, and I'd have to go and get the ladders, and blah, blah, blah, blah, *blah* . . . And finally she caved in:

'All right, all right – if you don't *want* to show me . . .'

I gave her a shit-eating grin.

'Let's go and have some dinner,' I said.

The smell of simmering veal wafted through the gap and drew her back into the kitchen. I held my hand against the light switch, and felt sweat trickling down my brow. I turned off the light, closed and locked the door, grabbed a tea towel, wiped my forehead, turned up the gas beneath the pan, and hung the key back on the hook. Then I followed her across the hall and into the living room.

This is what my living room looks like.

It's L-shaped, but in reverse. The base of the 'L' is a narrow passage leading from the hall; it's covered from floor to ceiling with Escher prints of various sizes, including all the ones I've attempted to carve on myself. This passage leads into the main part of the room. The walls throughout are white; the ceiling and carpets are red, which is pretty tasteless, but it's a hassle to redecorate when you're only renting short term.

At the far end, by the window overlooking the garden, there's a round dining table which extends to accommodate six people. Last night (and earlier this evening) it was covered with a white table cloth and twin white candles. Against the right wall, as you enter, there's an armchair (in the corner) and a mini hi-fi, with a coffee table in between. At this point in the story, Kate's sitting in that armchair, listening to the radio again . . . OK. Turn ninety degrees to the left. On the near wall there's a sofa, covered with a sort of stripy pattern. Vertical stripes. Thin, red and white. John calls it *The Psycho Zebra* . . . In the far corner, partly obscured by the dining table, is the television, beneath which I keep my collection of cartoon videos. *Tom and Jerry, Bugs Bunny, Roadrunner,* and – my favourite – *Daffy Duck.* On the facing wall, to the left of the armchair and opposite the sofa, there's a bookshelf. It runs from floor to ceiling and disguises an open fireplace.

These are just the bare details.

'Is there anything you want me to do?' Kate asked.

'More or less cooks itself from here,' I lied, worrying that I'd have to go and check the liquid level again, even though I'd only just inspected it. 'But, if you want, you can set the table for the first course.'

'Which is?'

'A surprise.'

We'd been together, on and off, for three months, and she was growing used to my surprises – to the point, in fact, where they no longer surprised her. Our conversation was still a little guarded, a bit too earnest at times; but the petals were unfolding . . . Anyway, she set the table while I checked the pan for the millionth time. Two plates, four knives, four forks, two spoons, and the bottle of wine. She also lit the candles. Small candle flames don't bother me; but I can never light a match without my hands shaking. By the time I returned, everything was ready.

'Are you going to tell me now?' she asked.

'About what?' I said, genuinely puzzled.

'Why you're afraid of fire.'

'I'll tell you after dinner. I don't want to spoil your appetite.'

'You *teaser* . . .' she complained. 'It's not *that* bad, surely?'

'No, not really.'

I went back to the kitchen, took the starter from the larder, and checked the osso buco again. It was fine, of course. When I placed the dish in front of her, I received a gratifying gasp of pleasure. Gratifying because I'd taken great care with the presentation: a pure white plate bordered and criss-crossed with thin, red, elliptical cuts of meat, and sprinkled with strips of green. It looked – as I intended, in memory of David – like a bicycle wheel.

'Looks nice,' she said, poking at one of the spokes. 'What is it?'

'Carpaccio with fresh basil,' I replied, rather grandly. 'Thin slices of raw beef . . .'

'I *know* what carpaccio is.'

'. . . marinated in olive oil, garlic, lemon juice. Basil leaves cut into strips. Salt and pepper—'

'It *is* safe, isn't it?' she interrupted.

I gave her a withering stare, and sat down.

This is what I see beyond the candle flame: Kate's thin, white face framed by long black hair. Her eyes, which I know are brown, appear black. She has slim, bloodless lips, a beak-like nose, pencil-thin eyebrows, short ears, a bird's neck. I can see the top of her bony shoulders too, and the rubber band biceps of her arms. Some people think she looks odd, but this strangeness is precisely what I find attractive about her; and I'm sure she feels the same way about me . . . But I've told you some of this before, and her appearance hasn't changed since.

Anyway, the thin white face swallows the thin slice of beef and comments, in all sincerity: 'That's *really* nice.'

'I'll give my compliments to the cow,' I say.

And I look into the candle flame and see the flame of The Burning. I see the dancing silhouettes: a man and a woman moving against each other. He's holding a weapon in his right hand, and she's cowering; and as he raises the weapon above his head, she raises her arms in defence. But he swings it down into her chest, and she crumples beneath him like paper crushed in a fist.

And he doesn't stop swinging. This is what worries me. He doesn't *stop*.

'What's up?' Kate asked.

'Nothing,' I said. I felt sick.

'You've got a face like a trout.'

'Well, thank *you*.'

'Don't mention it . . . Is it your food?'

'No.' I ran for cover, and found it. 'I just remembered something, that's all.' She waited for me to continue. 'D'you remember the first time we met?'

'How could I forget?' She laughed. 'I scared you to *death*.'

I should tell you – and I'm sure you won't be surprised – I didn't have thousands of girlfriends before Kate. I had four.

The first one was a mistake. They always are. She lasted about three weeks, all told, and she left me because of my phobia about mirrors. She *loved* mirrors. She couldn't understand why I wouldn't go near her when she was straightening her hair or shopping for clothes. And when I mentioned that I'd once considered using video cameras to see what mirrors do behind your back – well, she just thought I was *weird*. It's my own fault, of course. You should only be honest with people you trust . . . The second one lasted two days. She took one look at my butcher's equipment, and didn't call again. Our milestones included a trip to the cinema, one very long walk, and one long, penetrative kiss – my first . . . The third lasted the longest of all. Almost six months. The fact that she was on work placement abroad for the last five of these obviously contributed to the durability of our courtship. When she returned she didn't even want to see me, or talk to me on the telephone, despite the dozens of love letters I'd sent . . . The fourth (and the last one before Kate) was, like one of my current friends, called Alison. We were together for three weeks, and she asked a lot of questions, and I answered with a lot of lies. We reached what my doctor once delicately referred to as *the mutual masturbation phase*, and she almost discovered what I keep in the shortbread tin – but in the end, it was something much simpler which drove us apart. She was (and probably still is) a vegetarian.

As you can see, David's Skin hasn't been used to excess.

You may be wondering why I discussed sex with my doctor. Well, it's no big secret. My impostor-father persuaded me to see him for a few months after my mother left us, because I was having what the medical profession likes to describe (euphemistically) as *problems*. It didn't do me any good. He was an interfering old sod who just wanted to get off on someone else's misery, and I stopped going soon after I left home. End of story.

Kate finished the carpaccio. All of it. There are few things more flattering than someone eating something you cook for them. I took her plate, and said something like *I'll just check the main course hasn't burned to a crisp*, and then I nipped off to the kitchen.

The osso buco had almost dried out. It was a toss-up between adding more liquid (and waiting even longer), or serving it as it was with a thick, slightly rich sauce. I settled on serving it. Osso buco, as I'm sure you know, is knuckle of veal. I'd prepared it in the Milanese style, with plenty of tomatoes and white wine. It takes about two hours to cook, but the result is usually worth it. You get this beautiful, rounded, knobbly ball of bone and flesh, with borders of yellow fat, like a shoulder joint, smothered in a golden sauce.

'It's osso buco,' I explained to Kate. 'Veal knuckle.'

She looked faintly queasy.

'Most people can't face it at first.'

'What's in the sauce?'

I told her. 'Just try it. If you don't like it, I'll stick it in the fridge and eat it some other time.'

She was hesitant, as most people are when they're faced with something that looks more human than animal. Pure flesh and bone – food that isn't filleted, or sliced, or fried in breadcrumbs, or swamped by vegetables, or carved in some arty way – it's not for the squeamish. But she cut off a slice and swallowed.

'What d'you think?' I asked.

'Strange,' she said. 'It's not like I thought it would be.' She took another bite. 'Quite fatty, really.' And another. 'But I could get used to it.'

A euphemism for *I'd rather not have this again*; she left most of it on the plate, apologetically. I, on the other hand, ate the lot. Fat and flesh, sauce and herbs. Everything but the pure, white bone. And while we ate, we talked. About her, about me, about what we'd done, and what was happening in the world, and what ought to happen. As I took away her plate with its asteroid of bone, she apologized again.

'No problem,' I said.

It all began about three months ago. Much earlier, of course, if you count the girl on the beach, and the Joke Lighter Queen at the disco. But this is stuff you know. What you don't know is how we met recently.

It's quite simple. Like my friend Alison, Kate's a regular customer at the shop; but unlike Alison, she's always been served by me. She's what John and I refer to as a TCD, or *Typical Carnivore Diet*; which means that her buying habits are pretty unadventurous. Rashers of bacon, chicken fillets, joints of beef, that kind of thing. Anyway, over time we got to know each other: I'd recommend more unusual cuts of meat; she'd request advice on carving and preparation. We got to trust each other; we had a laugh . . . And these things build up. Before you know it, you're offering to come round and cook the pigs' trotters yourself.

From that moment on, there's no turning back. Not without pain. There's a spiral of involvement, and jealousy, and possession, and you can't escape it. You want to have and to hold and to *own*, exclusively. When she praises someone else, you want to stab that person through the heart and burn his house down and put a curse on his family for generations – I'm speaking for myself, of course. You want to be not just a part of her, and her a part of you, but to *absorb* her, draw her in until there are no differences. It's a violent and dangerous time – but it passes.

It passes, and one evening you find yourself sitting down, calmly exchanging secrets, eating carpaccio and osso buco, laughing.

*   *   *

When I served the dessert, she said, 'D'you mind if I smoke?'

And I almost said, *No, go ahead*, which might just have prevented the whole thing from ever happening. But instead I objected: 'To be honest: yeah.'

It was such an arresting reply, I had to cover it with a mock grimace, and then I had to explain. And as I explained, the story about The Burning slithered out from its deep hole, and sneaked up behind me, and tapped me on the shoulder; and suddenly it was there, demanding to be told. So I obliged it, repeating everything but the vision behind the flames: the toy train, the cot, the telephone conversation, the heat of the fire, the burning clothes, the sink with its vortex of water draining away. And she ate dessert – homemade amarena ice-cream, with amarena cherries – and drank coffee; and I couldn't help but notice the ironic contrast between the cold food she was eating and the heat in the story. (A trivial detail, but I'm pleased to have seen it.)

By the time I'd finished, and she'd stopped asking questions, the table was almost empty, the candles half-burned. I cleared away the plates and threw them in the sink. She helped me wash and dry.

'What time do you have to go?' I said.

And she replied: 'I don't have to go at all.'

A dance followed. An ancient and very formal dance, in which each partner knows the steps without reference to a manual or a teacher. We went through all the movements, all the expressions, and delivered all our lines correctly. But the words are the least important part. The angle and depth of the smile, the dilation of the pupils, the mutual, self-contained attention, the use of the hands and tongue – these are the marks by which the dance is recognized.

After an hour, we took a break. No words were exchanged, but we knew it was only the beginning. She kissed me and went to the bathroom, and I watched her from the doorway as she unpacked her handbag: five unknown tubes and bottles, a hair brush, a yellow plastic duck, a plastic container of skin cream, and a round, blue tin (like a tiny waste bin) decorated with transfers of rabbits.

'*You* came prepared,' I said.

'It's one of my two mottoes,' she replied. 'The other one is: *Never let anyone watch you removing your face*.' She closed the door, and all I could see through the frosted glass was a blur extending its hands towards its head.

I removed her coat from the bed and threw it onto the morning chair by the front window; then I undressed, put on my pyjamas (red, of course), and wrapped up a few necessary tools in a hand towel. I heard the bathroom door open, and we passed in the hallway, embracing and dancing a little more before reversing roles.

In the bathroom I examined all the items she'd brought along. I unscrewed the lid of the skin cream and tasted it (it was oily, and unpleasant). Then I prised open the top of the blue tin (and discovered half a dozen tampons), looked for hairs on the hair brush (there weren't any), and picked up the plastic duck and squeezed it (air wheezed from a small hole in the bottom).

Having satisfied my curiosity, I unrolled the hand towel, removed the Scalpel, opened one of the foil packs, and slid the fresh blade onto the handle. Then I took the mirror down from the wall, balanced it against the cistern, sat on the toilet lid, and pulled up my pyjama top. With the Scalpel in my right hand, and sitting at an angle, I adjusted the mirror until it gave an adequate reflection of bare skin . . . And when the preparations were done, I spoke the words and carved the flesh. A simple knife icon just above the left shoulder blade. The pain was far from overwhelming – certainly when I compare it to this evening – but it was enough to concentrate my mind and clarify the vision I'd seen . . . But I can't say I enjoyed the discovery. At first I thought it must be an illusion, or a lie. But it was not an illusion. It was not a lie.

I cleaned up, stuck plasters on the wounds, and wrapped the tools in the towel again. Then, after checking that all the lights were out and all the doors were locked, I returned to the bedroom.

The light was on, and Kate was lying there, coiled beneath the duvet, like a snake with the head of a smiling child.

'Do you mind if I turn out the light?' I asked.

'If you want,' she said.

The snake was swallowed by darkness, and I walked slowly around the bed to the far side, guided by the stored pattern of the room inside my head. I sat down on the edge. (Incidentally, you should know that darkness or light makes little practical difference in my bedroom: the walls and ceiling are black, the carpet is black, the curtains are black, with a dyed black lining, the bed is painted black, with a black headboard, and the duvet is *mainly* black. You can talk about regression and neo-pseudo-crypto-wombs if you want – but I chose the colour scheme simply because it seemed appropriate, and Kate loved it because it mirrored her depressive tendencies, and that's all that matters.)

Well, anyway: then it began.

She put her arm on my waist, and pulled me down towards her. She was naked. Clean skin. Pure, like David's . . . I stroked her hair. Kissed her. She unbuttoned my pyjama shirt, and I lay down next to her; and she lifted herself on top of me, holding my face as she kissed my eyelids. When I opened them again my eyes had adjusted to the gloom, and her head was a white moon, a spinning moon, a spinning wheel, a wheel of fire, a flame . . . Then in one quick movement, she rolled me over and raised me above her, loosening the plasters on my back. She eased my shirt off, casting it into the dark like a skin. She ran her fingers down my spine. She found the wound on my shoulder.

And she stopped.

'You're still wet . . . It's running down your back.'

I said nothing, hoping she would continue. I was so close.

'Ugh . . . it's *thick*. Sticky.'

'Soap,' I said. 'Forget it.'

Briefly, we began again. As we kissed she began to remove my pyjama bottoms, wiping her wet fingers on the material. Somewhere deep inside me there was a small, quiet laugh . . . But we were naked together. Elemental. Bodies of fire and earth, gasps of air, skins of sweat. In my ecstasy, I saw swinging sides of beef, and bags of bones, and the wonderful, round rims of the offcuts bins. And in the roundness of her round moon face, and in her round breasts, and in her round nipples, and in her navel, I saw the spinning wheels of David's bicycle arcing high in the air, spinning, spinning.

And *I* stopped.

After a moment, she stopped, too. 'What is it?' she asked. When I didn't reply, she pulled me gently down towards her and said, 'It's OK, it's OK . . . It doesn't matter . . . It's OK.'

But it wasn't OK.

I withdrew from her, and kissed her, and went to the bathroom. The sound of footfalls and the hum of the freezer. Switching on the light, I squinted, then looked down at my limp penis. It was coated in a thin, patchy film of blood.

When I returned, she embraced me tightly in the darkness, and stroked my back, so gently. I wanted to pull away, but I couldn't. Her affection succeeded where our sex had failed: it held me there. But her fingers found the ridged wounds on my back, as I knew they would . . . And she had to ask:

'What's this?'

The small laugh that had been trapped within me escaped. But nothing could spoil this moment, this intimacy. 'Ask me tomorrow,' I said. 'It'll take too long to explain now. It's nothing to worry about.'

She pulled me closer, and didn't let go, and after a while I heard her breathing deeply.

But I stayed awake for over an hour to make sure that she was asleep.

16

That night, which was last night, I had a dream.

It wasn't one of those long dreams, where you live your entire life again or (worse still) have to put up with someone else's; nor was it an upsetting dream, as many are, where you wake up crying, and even though you know it was only a dream you can't stop yourself feeling miserable. It wasn't particularly surreal, or mundane, or neurotic either; and it definitely *wasn't* a nightmare. Unfortunately, it was my least favourite dream of all. It was sexual.

I record my dreams in a little red book which I keep hidden under the mattress. I don't know who I'm hiding it *from* exactly, but you never know when someone might just wander in, and find the book lying there, and read it, and then they'll probably go thinking it's all the truth, and before you know it they've got the police round, and you're being carted off, complaining *it was all a fantasy, none of it's true* . . . Anyway, the point is, I wrote down last night's dream while Kate was in the bathroom this morning.

Is it Significant?

How should *I* know?

This is what I remember.

It's midday, and I'm standing behind a pillar box near the market; and I'm hiding, because two people are sardined in an embrace nearby, and I don't want to embarrass them. They both have long black hair, and they're wearing jeans, so at first I can't tell who's who or what's what. It doesn't seem to matter. They're so mutually absorbed they might as well be one person . . . Well, eventually, I get bored, and wander back off to work – but the couple follow me, still pressed together in that embrace, shuffling sideways like a crab, and as I approach the entrance to the market, they swing in front of me and bar the way.

I begin to abuse them verbally, but they refuse to budge, and the only way I can pass is by thrusting my hand between them and prising their bodies apart. This, it turns out, is the wrong thing to do. As they separate, the male half of the couple quite literally *spills* onto the pavement: his skin collapses like an empty sack, and he dissolves into a pool of blood and lumps of offal. The female half, on the other hand, is unaffected. She looks at me, and I look at her, and she doesn't recognize me, but I know who *she* is. It's Kate – and just as I'm about to ask her what she's doing kissing a stranger, and a boneless one at that, she runs away, screaming with all the air in her lungs: *Murderer!*

She heads into the market, and I follow: no one is listening to her cries, so I'm in no hurry. I see her, always just ahead, dancing and skipping, twisting and turning through the narrow alleyways, looking for a way out . . . But there are no exits here; and the only open door she finds leads into my butcher's shop. I track her inside, only to discover that she's disappeared. She's not in front of the serving counter, or behind the partition, or under the table, or anywhere . . . But the white door to the cold store is open.

The cold store looks like my mother's chest freezer turned on its edge, and as soon as I pass over its threshold, I discover that it's dimly lit, terribly cold, and unimaginably large inside. It seems to extend for half a mile or more ahead, and just as far to the right and left, and there are hundreds of long, parallel steel poles running just above head height, on which sides of pork and quarters of beef are hanging from gambrels. The meat is swinging, slowly. Cut bones. Stone-hard flesh. Everything spotted with frost. But Kate is still nowhere to be seen. I shout for her, but the sound is absorbed by the meat.

A finger taps me on the shoulder. I spin around, and there's no one there, but I feel a hand on my back, and a voice says: 'Welcome to the house of hair pie.' It's Kate's voice, but I can't see her and I don't understand what she's saying. 'Butcher's window. Bacon sandwich. Mutton.' The voice begins to fade. 'Chopped liver. Honeypot. Jellybox.' I chase after her, calling for her to come back, and in the distance I can hear her voice, echoing: 'Golden doughnut. Fish. Slice of life.'

The sounds recede into silence, and I stop chasing her, exhausted.

I feel a tap on the shoulder again.

When I turn around, there's still no one there, but the rocks of frozen meat are swinging violently. The gambrel sticks rub against the poles, squeaking and juddering with the weight of the beef and pork. One of the sides brushes against me, chafing the skin. I back away, a reflex action, but a long red punchbag of pig hits me square in the side, knocking me over. I hit my head on the stone floor, and pass out; and when I come to, Kate is supporting me in her lap, stroking my hair. The meat is swinging gently again, but from where I'm lying it appears that the background is motionless, and that Kate's upside-down head is moving. I feel nauseous, and close my eyes.

'It's OK,' she says. 'It doesn't matter.'

'It does matter,' I tell her. 'It *does*.'

We're both naked, and it's so cold. I look at her breasts, her pubic hair, her long, thin legs. Her pure white flesh, streaked with frost; her long, black hair, with white flecks of ice. We stand up together, and the light grows dimmer still, and we're surrounded by a dark, organic world of red and brown blurs. It's like someone has taken dusk and frozen it solid. But there are still some carcasses swinging, and there are reflected glints of silver light from the metal poles and hooks, like the spangle of a mirrorball on a dance floor . . . Kate puts her arms around me and asks me to hold her – softly, as if the frost itself is whispering. I'm a shadow in the darkness, and I put my arm around her waist, lowering her gently to the ice floor. There's no violence. I'm a shadow, and I climb on top of her, at first to keep her warm; then I move with increasing vigour as my body takes over. I'm a shadow, and I roll with her beneath the meat, speeding into a spin of white flesh and black hair, a whirling blur of connected meat.

When the spinning stops I'm alone again; but there's a leech frozen to the floor next to me. I reach out to crush it with my fingers, but it somehow frees itself and slips away. Then I try to grab hold of it, but it eludes my grasp again and again, and all the time it's growing larger. It fills with blood, swelling to four or five times its previous size. (Well, it's obvious enough to me *now* what this is all about, but the dream wasn't giving any secrets away then.) And while I've been trying to trap the leech, the light has grown brighter, and I see that the hanging carcasses have been transformed. Swinging from the gambrels are – get this – thousands of naked *groins* . . . Some male, some female. On each there's no body above the waist, and there are no legs below the thighs, and the skin is completely bald. Cold, white, bloodless joints, hanging there like misshapen moons. And I feel briefly as if I can conquer the world; but my satisfaction soon shrinks to regret, which shrivels to guilt, which withers to disgust . . . I glance down at the leech, which has crawled onto my leg and is extending its nine-inch nose into my thigh. I tickle its belly repeatedly, hoping it will fall off, but it simply bursts in a shower of blood.

And this isn't the worst of it. A moment later, all those neatly-trimmed carcasses hanging from the gambrels above my head, all those rocks of *flesh* burst open, too. It's disgusting. It's fascinating and funny. It's like a thousand water bombs exploding, covering me with a thousand showers of warm, red rain.

. . . At this point I woke up, hungry, and with an erection. And I remembered immediately what I'd done the night before – about the sex, I mean. And that led to guilt. Which meant a Rite of Exposure. (The sequence is unavoidable.)

I reached an arm over the bed to embrace Kate, but (as in my dream) she wasn't there. It was daylight. The black bedroom walls looked cheap and dirty. I heard the sound of running water from the bathroom, and a deep gurgle as it disappeared down the plug hole. Then the toilet flushing. I lay face down on her side of the bed, where it was still warm, and closed my eyes. After a while, when dozing was giving me a headache, I sat up, reached for the book of dreams, and wrote down everything I've just told you.

Kate spent *years* in the bathroom, but at last I heard the sound of footsteps in the hall. I leapt out of bed, found my balance, and opened the bedroom door. She was standing there, in the doorway, with a clean, scrubbed face and wet hair, wearing my dressing gown.

'Good *morning*,' I said, as cheerily as possible.

She stared at the ridged scars on my torso for a long time – but if she was horrified, as anyone in her position would have had every right to be, she didn't show it much. Perhaps what she saw connected with something deep inside her, some darkness that was part of her, too. She reached out a hand and let it rest on the devil's head on my chest, running her fingers along the raised white flesh, following the outline through the black hairs.

'Do they hurt?' she asked.

'Not any more,' I told her. I realized she must have been thinking about the scars, if not all night, then certainly since she'd woken up. Maybe she'd even looked at them while I was asleep? 'They hurt at first. But the pain goes away after a while.'

She wanted to know *why*. I could see it. But she didn't know how to frame the question so it would sound reasonable, and unintrusive, and safe. Above all, *safe*. She wasn't frightened, though. Instead she changed the subject.

'I heard you laughing while you were asleep.'

'Oh yeah?'

'Yeah. It must have been a sweet dream. You sounded like a child. All happy.'

'I can't remember why,' I lied.

We stared at each other in silence.

'I'll just go to—' I began; but she interrupted.

'Will you tell me about them?' she said. 'The scars, I mean.'

'After breakfast,' I replied. 'If you promise not to laugh and point.'

'I won't,' she said, unnecessarily. 'But I'm interested. I don't want to be nosey. I'd just like to know *why*.'

'Of course,' I said. 'You've got a right to know. I should have told you before.'

We parted in the corridor . . . and this is probably the *key* moment. If she hadn't done what she did, it might have been all right, and we might have got on well together – as friends at first, and in time, who knows? She could have helped. She could even have stopped me.

But she didn't. She fucked it up.

We both did.

So. We parted in the corridor. She disappeared into the bedroom and closed the door, to keep the draught out. She didn't look at my back. It would have been OK if she had: I think she was beginning to understand. I heard a hairdryer, which I hadn't seen her smuggle in (she was full of surprises). I went into the kitchen first, and took down the red tartan shortbread tin from the shelf. The Skin rattled around inside, briefly. At this point in the ceremony I always keep the tin closed. It stays that way until I reach the place where the Rite of Exposure is due to take place, partly as an observance, but also because opening the lid releases a peculiar, musty stench, a combination of preserving fluid and age. If you're expecting visitors, you don't want this smell all over the house.

Once I was safely in the bathroom I locked the door behind me, placed the tin carefully on the shelf, and removed my pyjama bottoms. My penis was still erect, something which Kate had noticed but not remarked on. I sat down on the toilet lid, took the tin and opened it, removing the soft, walnut oblong of flesh with my right hand. I put the container on the floor and ran my fingers over the short, brittle hairs on the flesh. In the distance, the hairdryer switched off: I wasn't going to have much time . . . The mirror was next. I took it down from the wall and balanced it at an angle against the cistern, so that when I stood up I could see the reflection of my erect penis. I caught a glimpse of the fine pink and white scars on my face, from The Burning, and was reassured about abstract concepts which won't mean much to you unless you, too, have lived a life by ritual: *wholeness, tradition, rightness.* The complete picture is much more complex, but these are its primary colours.

I put on my glasses, which I'd left in the bathroom overnight, so that I could see clearly what I was doing, and ensure that the positions were precise, the movements correct. Taking the Skin in both hands, I held it out at arm's length, turning it over so that all the details could be seen; then raised it to my nostrils, inhaling the rich odours. These are not what they used to be – there's no longer a sweet smell of meat, or an odour of blood. Every ritual demands a sacrifice, and this ritual has taken the life from its own magic object. Still, it's the Significance of the icon which counts, not its appearance. Everyone knows this.

And it was time to begin, in a whisper, in a whisper:

I feel the ghost of blood and bone. I feel the muscle and the flesh. Our skins are one. It is ended and begun.

I rubbed the Skin, hair side, on my cheeks, first the left, then the right, relishing the rough, prickling sensation. Then I turned it over, so that the raw side (what *was* the raw side –

it's no longer literally so) was pressed against my face, and did the same again. I repeated the action for my chest, first the left half, then the right, at either side of the devil's head. Then again for my stomach; and the bicycle scar on my left calf; and both my buttocks, left and right as before. When this was over I stood completely still and silent for a couple of seconds, as was customary.

I was about to perform the final act in the ritual. I turned David's Skin over in my hands, letting it lightly touch the wrinkled white scars of The Burning which ran along the wrist, over the palm, and down towards the hooked fingers. Then I balanced it at the base of my erect penis and concentrated on the memory of his bare, uncut chest. His purity. My impurity. The day at the canal. The dam, and his strong arms. His face in the darkness of the upturned oil tank. The spinning wheels . . . And the blood drained from my penis, slowly, slowly.

It was almost over.

But she fucked it up. I heard footsteps running down the hallway, then a loud knock on the door.

'What *are* you doing in there?' It was Kate, feigning impatience.

But I didn't recognize the feint. I panicked, and grabbed hold of the Skin, and threw it under the towel on the chair. If I'd thought for just one more second, I would have tossed it back into the shortbread tin and closed the lid. I could have explained *that* quite easily. But my judgement was clouded. I was terrified of being found out.

She pushed at the door. Bless that lock.

'What's that *smell?*' she said – and this time the curiosity was genuine.

I had some explaining to do.

17

It's important that I describe to you *precisely* what happened next, but first I need to mention my fifth and final friend – Nigel.

Nigel is not at all what you would expect, given his name alone. Well, perhaps you see no significance in a name, and you expect *nothing*. Whatever. I've known him for only a year, and in all that time he's only ever worn any one of half a dozen varicoloured V-neck sweaters, ditto varicoloured deck shoes, ditto varicoloured socks, ditto varicoloured slacks. I don't *know* the colour of his underpants, but I expect they're varicoloured too. He's worn this outfit summer and winter, with only one concession to variety: he sometimes wears nothing beneath the jumper, preferring to reveal his hairless chest . . . So where did we meet? I remember: I first spoke to him in an antiques shop. Like Alison and me, he too is a collector – but his passion is for astronomical memorabilia. Old brass astrolabes, sextants, telescopes, binoculars, nocturnals, star charts – that kind of thing. On his living room wall he's got a reproduction of the plaque sent into space aboard Pioneers 10 and 11. It perhaps won't surprise you to learn that his major ambition is to find a replica of Kepler's three-dimensional model of the solar system – the one based on geometric principles. (No, I didn't know about it, either.) Some people laugh at this obsession, but I say *at least he hasn't killed anyone.* Oh – and one more thing: I think he was a mathematics student at some college somewhere but, as with many snippets of information whirling around inside my head, I can't say for sure.

Though it caused no lasting damage, his is the silliest and most futile accident of all, if you can talk that way about misfortune. It happened four months ago, which makes it by far the most recent of the accidents, and served to fully inaugurate Nigel into our social circle . . . We were all having dinner at Alison's house, and he produced one of the most surreal moments of spontaneity I've ever witnessed. We were having an argument, which became increasingly heated – it might even have led to terminal bitterness had Nigel not done what he did – but just when the level of shouting became unbearable, he leapt onto the dinner table, breaking a couple of plates in the process, curled into a squat, and began to leap up and down like a frog, blowing raspberries until everyone was silent. Having achieved this, he quietly climbed off, put on his coat, and said: 'I'll see you all next week.' Anyway, we spent the rest of the evening talking about him, and forgot all about our disputes. Unfortunately – and I *am* finally getting to the accident itself – fifteen minutes later he crashed blindly into a ditch and was rushed to the hospital, where he received five stitches in his forehead.

There's no justice, is there?

18

That's all you need to know about my friends.

Except for Kate. Kate never suffered a cycling accident. We all joked about how it would be nice if she could arrange one for herself. It didn't have to be anything drastic, like a wheel collapsing, or a collision with a train, or what happened to Nigel. We would have been happy with a puncture followed by a nasty fall. But there it is. It's too late now.

OK. There are three strands I've still got to unravel: Kate, the dinner party, and what happened to me this evening. I'll begin where I left off a couple of minutes ago.

She knocked on the bathroom door again, and I stalled with something like *Wait a minute*, and she repeated that mocking tone with a *What's going on in there?* and I gave her some facetious comment like *I'm just cutting my head off but the saw-teeth keep getting stuck*, and she said, quite seriously, *Well hurry up, I want some breakfast* . . . I don't recall the exact dialogue. I was so scared of sharing this small secret about David's Skin that I went completely limp almost immediately, and couldn't concentrate on anything else. Fortunately, I remembered to pull on my pyjama bottoms before opening the door.

'So it was all a lie about cutting your head off,' she said, dryly.

'Depends which head you're talking about,' I quipped, not displeasingly.

My face was hot and red, which she didn't pick up on, or at least she pretended not to. I think she thought I'd been playing with myself. I tried to ease by her, but she stopped me gently with her hand.

'Felix . . . What *is* that smell?'

'Look,' I said, thinking fast. 'I've got a guilty secret.' She stared at me, puzzled. Frank, open face. 'I've got dandruff. You know – flaky white scalp, scabs, the lot. And scurvy. Ascorbic acid deficiency.' The words rolled off my lips. 'Look at my gums.' I flashed my teeth at her, and she backed off: the memory of last night's osso buco was too much. 'I rub the shampoo into my scalp, the dandruff disappears. I eat fresh fruit and vegetables, the gums don't—'

'Yeah, yeah,' she interrupted. 'What is it *really*?'

I didn't say anything. It was none of her business, after all. And I think she got the message, because her face screwed up into a frown, her lips pouting like a dog's sphincter, and she said:

'I sometimes don't know when you're telling the truth.'

'I always tell the truth, and I always lie,' I replied. It sounded clever, but I couldn't quite figure out *why* exactly. I'm not sure even now.

There was an air of bitterness between us for some while afterward, but the moment of danger had passed without significant trouble . . . Except, of course, that I forgot all about the dried Skin beneath the towel. Well, as my real father used to say, *You can remember everything so long as you don't remember the things that you've forgotten.*

And that *is* the truth.

Later that morning, after a silent and slightly hostile breakfast, which was just toast and jam and coffee, she said,

'Are you going to show me the scars *now*?'

I needed to say sorry, and she knew it. I should have given her a straight answer about the Skin, and my evasiveness had hurt her feelings. And I *could* have done it, if I'd prepared the ground beforehand – people will understand anything if you tell them at the right time. For now, though, I had to deal with the Cutting; so I answered her question with an invitation:

'D'you want to have a bath together? I can show you then.'

And she thought about it, and fought against it for some time; but I could see the hint of a smile wriggling at the edge of her mouth, and finally she agreed. All couples have dark secrets which unite them, and self-mutilation was *our* special bond: I had my rituals, she had the barcode on her wrist. Perhaps, in the end, she just wanted to see how similar we were, or – more likely – how *different*. Maybe she needed to see how far I'd gone so that she could feel better about her own cutting.

'Good,' I said. 'I'll get some of the food ready for tonight first – you can give me a hand, if you want – and then we'll do it.'

She nodded, and I could feel her fingers already itching to run along the pink and white ridges again, to explore the curves and angles and spirals of the marks, to see, in the daylight, the shapes that her touch inferred last night. And my flesh bristled with anticipation.

After some more boring stuff in the bedroom (only ten minutes this time), we both got dressed and went into the kitchen to decide what needed to be done. We couldn't make any of the starters – John was bringing the pigs' feet and pork scratchings, and the sausages didn't have to be prepared until later in the morning at the earliest – so I began by making the stuffing for the head. Coarse sausage meat, pork tongues, cubed ham, hard boiled eggs, pistachios, seasoning. I assigned Kate the task of chopping up the ingredients for the soup, including the leftover veal knuckle from last night, some lean beef, a few leeks, celery, carrots, pepper, and so on. The head, by the way, used to belong to a boar. The soup was consommé.

This preparation took a couple of hours, and we didn't talk much. Well, nothing relevant, anyway. I'd like to say we shared the sort of bland pleasantries that two people about to be involved in a killing would; but the conversation didn't have any kind of edge whatsoever. We played a few word-games, talked about what we were going to have for dinner, discussed when everything had to be ready, what we were going to do tomorrow, how her family was, exchanged memories of childhood, made sarcastic remarks about the weather, exercised a few tired puns. No one is to blame for shallowness. It just happens.

OK, OK. *One* example:

'Aren't you working today?' Kate asked. She was chopping up a leek.

'No,' I said. 'It's John's shift this weekend.'

I was paring the meat off the veal knuckle for her. For some reason, she couldn't face it.

At about eleven-thirty we decided to have lunch. We'd been preparing food for almost two hours. (Lazily, of course: anyone who says it takes a couple of hours to slice a few pieces of meat and chop a few vegetables is pulling a fast one.) I switched on the hot water for the bath and cleaned up some of the mess while Kate assembled a Greek salad. We ate in the living room, sitting opposite each other on the floor . . . And halfway through, I swore aloud.

'What's up?' Kate asked. (A crumb of feta was lodged in her teeth.)

'I should have done the sausages this morning,' I told her. (I visualized the casings in the larder, loose like condoms stretched beyond their elastic limit. I'd only need one, but I'd have to soak it first.)

'There's plenty of time,' she said. 'We'll do it after the bath. Have you got all the stuff?' (She always took an interest in what I was doing. It was habitual. Even when you could tell she didn't really care either way. Like with the Collection.)

I shook my head. 'That's what's bugging me. I've got to soak the skins first, and cook the meat, then leave it all to cool off. And they're supposed to be one of the starters.'

'Forget it,' she said, calmly. 'There's loads of time after lunch. You can always go out and buy some if it comes to it.'

We smiled at each other.

Tra la la.

After lunch, I ran the hot water into the bath and we undressed together in the bedroom. And in case you're wondering, we *didn't* have sex. Kate was more interested in my scars; and after last night, I didn't feel like going that far either. I just posed for her, naked, and let her inspect me.

She asked me if I'd seen *The Illustrated Man*. I haven't – I hardly ever watch television these days. So she explained that it was a film starring Rod Steiger, and he plays this character who's got tattoos on his skin which reveal stories and predict the future; but he doesn't call them tattoos, he calls them *skin ill-yu-strayshuns*. And the thought began to form in my head – as thoughts sometimes do when you realize you've been living a fiction which is very close to your own life, and without even knowing it – that I was like that. *I* was the Illustrated Man . . . But Kate went on to explain all the ways in which I *wasn't* like him. Some stuff about a witch who'd cursed him, and how he was a stranger wandering the roads, and it was all based on a loose collection of Ray Bradbury stories anyway; and I'd carved my*self*, of course, and *my* designs lacked the wild, shimmering colours of the film, and on and on until I was sick of her pedantic comparisons. In the end I made some remark about the bath being ready, and we abandoned the inspection.

With all that talking I'd forgotten to turn on the cold tap, and the bath was full to the brim with scalding water. Kate stuck her big toe in and burnt it, pulling back with a squeal, like a pig. (It was her left foot, if that's any use in helping you imagine the scene. And here are some more details: a steam-filled bathroom, a window – about to be opened – the dominant red linoleum and burgundy bath, the red towels on the chair and towel rail, and two naked people.) So, I opened the window to let out the steam, and then did something rather childish. I plunged my hand, up to the elbow, into the bath, and yanked out the plug, fighting back the agony of burning which leapt up the nerves in my arm. The water began to drain away, and I turned on the cold tap to try and equalize the temperatures. My arm ached, and I held it under the cold flow as the bath refilled. My hooked hand was a neat shade of boiled lobster, or rare steak, with a fine marbling of scars from The Burning.

'That was *stupid*,' Kate said matter-of-factly.

'It doesn't hurt,' I lied. 'My hands aren't all that sensitive. Not since the accident.' To prove it I replaced the plug with my other hand. The water wasn't as hot this time, but it still stung.

And there was pleasure there, too. Excess brings its own pleasure.

Kate lowered herself in at the taps end – gingerly, because the temperature was still a little too hot. I joined her, raising the water level to the brim: we had to keep absolutely still, our legs intertwined, until some of it drained away. I'd never done this before, and I didn't ask her if she had, so it was all a bit embarrassing. We washed separately, self-consciously, until at last she summoned the courage to raise my left foot in her hand and study the faint white scar.

'It's supposed to be a rabbit's foot,' I explained. She didn't reply, but traced its outline with her finger. I felt exposed by her examination. The nakedness didn't trouble me – it wasn't *me*. But the scars *were*. It was like she'd opened me up and turned me inside out.

'The thing that bothers me is *why* . . .' She faltered. 'I mean, why did you do it? I can see *what* you've done – it's – I don't know what to say – but what made you cut yourself? There must be a reason.'

So I explained. Slowly. Carefully. Not everything, and not

the whole truth. But enough to make me regret it. I said something about a *need* to do it, to release the pressure. My body – my mind – was like a pressure cooker. And it was like the blood was all the anger and the anguish inside, and when I released it, when I opened the valve in the skin, the bad blood and the tension escaped, and everything returned to normal, and I could *be* normal . . . And she nodded, because she *knew* how it was. But she wanted to know why I'd carved designs, and not just lines, like everyone else. So I said:

'There's always a reason for the pressure. When I copy the image of that reason onto my skin, it's like I'm exorcizing it.'

She smiled slightly. 'You seem to have it all worked out.'

Then she wanted to know the story behind each design, starting with the mirror-image head on my right foot.

'I just didn't feel too good about myself. I didn't feel too good about the image, either. It's not very accurate.'

The Lorenz attractor:

'My life wasn't going where I wanted it to. It was too complex and chaotic. So this is – *was* – a symbol. It has its own internal order, but it's hard to understand.'

The tessellation of hexagons and triangles on the back of my left thigh:

'I was bored.'

The dragon:

'It reminds me of my father.'

And so it went on. A bluff about the razor blade. A fictional account of the mirror reflecting the kite and my real father's face. Bullshit about the juggling balls, the Harborth's tiling sunflower, the Devil-God; and so on. Some of it was the truth, because some of the truth was innocent; but mostly it was invention. And all the time I had to twist and turn and stand up and sit down so that she could see all of the scars; and I felt ridiculous and ashamed.

And she pretended to be concerned. On the surface, of course. But I began to suspect that there was something behind it all, behind all the sympathy and the interest. Some controlling agent. Eventually, I saw what it was. It was that tiny worm again, the one I'd seen yesterday, burrowing beneath her brow. It pulled her skin tight, raising the flesh from her chin to her lips, bending her mouth downwards, almost imperceptibly. And it was on the move. I saw it pass behind her eyes, and suck the life from them. I saw it work its way into her tongue, controlling the responses, not letting her brain have its way. Her brain wanted to shout *Horror* and *Maniac*, but the worm had the power, and it said, *Really?*, and *That's interesting*, and *Tell me more*. (This is the way worms behave. You let them in, as a kindness, and they just take over. They destroy everything.) It even forced her to touch my skin, to follow the outlines of the scars with her fingers. It said to her, *Go ahead, I'll treat you. Have a good feel. But make sure you're back before nightfall, or there'll be hell to pay.* And I let her do it. I just licensed her roving hands and let them go. It was like a medical examination. Rubber hands and no emotion.

Then again – and I'm frightened to think of this now – maybe she really *was* curious. We both had a taste for the unusual. It would make sense. And why else would she have stayed so long? Either way, it was fine – just about. I kept the whole truth to myself (you have to; you lose your identity otherwise), and she kept her feelings locked inside.

So how did we get from that moment to this? Where did the argument come from?

The answer is: *the shoe.*

*   *   *

I stepped out of the bath onto the burgundy rug, dripping. I should have smuggled out the Skin there and then, but she was watching me. *The worm* was watching me. She should have got out before me, but the worm said it wanted her to wash her hair, because it had got greasy again after preparing all that food. So what can you do? You can't say, *Look, I've got this terrible secret hidden under that towel over there – you can probably smell it – and I'd rather you didn't see it. So, if you don't mind . . .* There's a point at which you just have to let the events take their course. So I did nothing. I just left, and made sure she had two dry towels hanging on the door, and splashed water on the towel on the chair just to make sure she wouldn't use it.

I got dressed and returned to the kitchen to prepare the ingredients for the sausages. I hadn't pre-minced the pork at work yesterday, so I had to chop it very fine. After that, it was time to use the Third Object, which I keep in the hallway, on the lower shelf. It's quite small but very heavy – cast-iron. It's a beautiful machine. I don't know exactly when it was made – there's no date-stamp – and it's probably not worth anything now because I had it adapted to run off the mains. All the original models were water- or air-powered, and there were three capacities: 20lbs, 50lbs and 100lbs. Mine's the smallest, and it's the type which uses water to flush out the main cylinder after every operation. It's a bit pointless when you're preparing small amounts of meat, but I like to indulge myself . . . And Kate came out of the bathroom just as I was lifting it off the shelf.

'What's that?' she asked. She was drying her hair on one of the large towels I'd left on the door.

'The Butcher Boy Electric Sausage Filler,' I announced grandly.

'Oh.'

She returned to the bedroom.

I carried the Sausage Filler into the kitchen and plugged it in. The rusk and the skins needed soaking first, and soaking is a precise process. Soak the casings too long and the meat runs out; don't soak the rusk for long enough and the sausages burst when you cook them. And if you plan to do this at home, try and get hold of Beef Weasands for the casing. There's nothing like them.

Forgive me. I have a story to tell.

The shoe hit me square in the back, just as I was cutting open the packet of casings with my knife. It was a soft throw, so there wasn't much pain, but (obviously) it distracted me. I turned around, and Kate was standing in the doorway. But for a bare left foot she was fully clothed. Blue tracksuit trousers with two large pockets, white T-shirt. One pocket had something in it, about the size of a child's hand. Her hair was still damp.

'What was that for?' I said.

'Because you're a liar!' she shouted. She rushed over to me, and at first I thought she was going to fly at me with her fists, but instead she picked up the shoe and slipped it back onto her foot. 'You're a bloody liar. You pretend you're telling the truth, but there's always something more. Always something you're holding back. And it's *sick*.' I knew I shouldn't have told her about the scars. Or about The Burning, for that matter. It always ends this way. The cycle reasserts itself: fear and self-loathing, ephemeral relief, then regret. But she hadn't finished. The worm had plenty more to say for itself, and it was making the most of an easy ride: 'Everything you've told me . . . It was all a *lie*. I could see it in your eyes. The stuff about your hands – you told me the truth about that. At least,

I *think* you did. And because I swallowed that you thought you could make up a whole pack of lies about everything else.'

I stared at her, wide-eyed; but all I could say was: '*What?*'

'It's disgusting,' she said. 'All that stuff in those . . . those *boxes*. I can cope with the Scalpel blades. And the photographs. I could have happily left here for good, knowing that I'd almost got myself mixed up with a headcase . . . but the blood, and the books, for Christ's sake? What made you write all that stuff? What made you do it? What's wrong with you?' I didn't reply. Passive resistance. 'What's *wrong* with you?' This was screamed at me.

I twitched involuntarily. 'Nothing's wrong,' I said, pathetically. 'I did it all to myself, I haven't harmed anyone else . . . I . . . And in the end, it isn't any of your business.' I was calm, but all the time I was wondering when she'd sneaked a look at the Collection. It must have been this morning. She must have found the key. And stood on something. All while I was asleep.

But she was still standing here now. She must still have wanted to *know*. Every last detail.

'How could you let me sleep with you last night, with all of . . . *this?*' She waved her arms, but didn't elaborate. 'Don't you think you should see a doctor?'

I blew off steam: 'Why don't you *fuck off.*'

'Once you've explained what this is.' And she reached into her tracksuit pocket and pulled out David's Skin.

This changed things.

I know how the Skin seems – how it must seem to you – but it's been a part of my life since I was a child. It's completely normal to me; believe this if you believe nothing else. Any defence I offered for it would appear ludicrous, and would be disrespectful to David's memory. So I continued to lie:

'Nothing,' I said. 'Just a bit of old leather. I use it to clean the bathroom.'

And the bluff was useless. Stupid. It would have been obvious to anyone that what she was holding was a piece of pickled skin. It had *hairs*, for God's sake. And there's that smell of preserving fluid. And the fat . . . It looked like skin, it felt like skin, and the way I was staring at it, it couldn't have been anything else.

'Look,' she said firmly, 'I've had enough. I don't want to know whose this is, or where it came from, or why it's here. I'm just going to pick up my stuff and go.' Her level-headedness was admirable. She turned around, dropping the Skin into her pocket without thinking, then turned to face me again. There was a look of determination on her face, set hard like plaster. 'And *don't* try to stop me.'

She returned to the bedroom to collect her bag, then went to the living room to pick up her Lighter and some cigarettes. I wasn't watching her. I remembered exactly where she'd left everything. But when she entered the bathroom I followed her. Unfortunately – and it still amazes me that such a small detail can affect your future so profoundly – I was still holding the knife I'd used to open the casings.

I began by whining at her: 'Is there nothing I can do to make it right?'

And she spun around, her eyes narrow with anger. 'It's always about *you*, isn't it? Is there nothing *you* can do. You did it all to your*self*. *You* didn't harm anyone else. You're so . . . self-*obsessed*. Everything and everyone – you see them in two dimensions. You rip out the bits that reflect you, you pick on the details, and you don't see the whole thing. You think everything you do is important, and nothing is. *Nothing*.' She turned back to the shelf, to her packing, but almost immediately found something else to say. 'All these tiny things you think are significant – they're just proof you need help. You can't go on with this. You'll damage yourself.' There was a trace of kindness, perhaps even sympathy, in her tone – which I valued.

'Are you going to tell anyone?' I said.

'No. It's your problem. *You* sort it out.'

Her voice was calm, but I didn't believe her. Somewhere, at some time, I knew she'd tell someone. If *I* couldn't keep a secret, what hope did she have?

I left the bathroom and waited in the hall as she packed her things. I was confused. I knew I ought to let her go, but I wanted an assurance. Some way of making certain that she would never tell. It wasn't that I considered what I'd done, and what I was doing, to be particularly shameful. It's just that by exposing my secrets she would be exposing *me*. My Rites, my Objects, my Symbols, my Collection: these are the four elements which make me who I am. And I couldn't bear the thought that sometime, somewhere, they would be revealed to (and ridiculed by) someone else.

The idea of it made me desperate.

So I returned to the bathroom and stood in the doorway.

'What do you want?' she asked. No trace of panic. She still believed, as I did, that we were perfectly capable of negotiating our little problem.

'I can't let you go,' I told her. 'I've decided. There's no other solution.'

She calmly fastened her bag, then placed her hand on my shoulder. 'Don't be an idiot,' she said.

I didn't reply, but remained firm.

'Look,' she continued, calmly. 'I've just got to pick up my

coat, and then I'll be gone. I've got no interest in your secrets, or in seeing you or your stupid friends again. Is that clear?' She almost persuaded me . . . but she made the mistake of trying to push me out of the way. If she'd been telling the truth, why did she need to use force?

'I can't let you go,' I repeated. 'Not yet. We have to work something out first.'

And she went *apeshit*. She threw down her bag and flew at me with her fists and feet. I remained as passive for as long as I could before pushing her down onto the toilet seat. I knew it was the wrong thing to do, but I was already in so deep I had no choice but to go through with it. Anyway, we argued briefly, and there was a lot of shouting, but it was obvious that neither of us was going to convince the other of our point-of-view. In positions like that, there can only be a winner and a loser. There's no room for sensible compromise.

She played her hand first. Without blinking or flinching, she pulled David's Skin from her pocket again. For a moment I thought she was going to throw it at me, but she just took the Lighter from her bag and positioned her thumb over the wheel. This is the joke Lighter, remember. The Fourth Object, on the shelf, just there by the Sausage Filler. Anyway, I took this threat to mean that if I didn't do what she said, right now, the Skin would go up in flames. She knew what it meant to me, and she saw that I understood.

'Now get the *fuck* out of my way,' she shouted.

'I can't,' I said.

So she ignited the flame.

Well, I've told you this before in a different way, but I might as well tell you again now: the Lighter released a huge, yellow, flickering flame with darkness at its heart and defining its borders. It rumbled and whistled and whined to itself, so quietly, like a bird. I felt the heat of it, and my hands and the scars on my face began to itch, and my fingers began to shiver. But this wasn't the worst of it. I could see the flame licking at his Skin, at David's Skin. It started to blacken, and it smelled awful. I'll never forget that smell. And her white face leered behind it all, like a devil. But she wasn't smiling. She took no pleasure from the fire. She just held the flame there, and let it eat at my life and the one thing I'd loved.

I couldn't let it go on.

I knocked the Lighter from her hand, and held her wrist until she dropped the Skin. She tried to stamp on it, and kick me, but I grabbed it and threw it under the chair by the bath. Then I pushed the door shut behind me, and locked us in. When I looked at her again, her eyes were filled with hatred. No fear – just hatred.

I didn't know what to do, and I could quite easily have let her go even then – and faced the consequences – had I not looked in the mirror at that moment. It was fortunate that I did, because this is what I saw: the back of Kate's head (all black hair), my own face (distorted and cut in two by the crack in the glass), and the white wall behind us both. I say *fortunate*, because at that moment I caught my alter ego, from the other side of the mirror, trying to slip through the crack into this world. And I *know* it sounds crazy – but I *saw* it, and it was *there*. And it left only one thought in my mind: I couldn't let it escape. That would have been the end. So I swung the knife high in the air . . . And you know the rest. You know the thought-picture. I felt the knife sink into flesh and grate against bone. I felt something collapse beneath me like a burst paper bag, crying and gurgling like a baby. But I only needed to strike once. The vision had lied . . . And when things became clearer, when my head had stopped screaming, and when my voice had stopped screaming, too, I saw that Kate was lying on the floor at my feet.

I collapsed to the floor and cried. I don't know how long for.

OK. There's a small part of me which feels *she* must take some responsibility for what happened. She knew about Pandora, about Bluebeard's wife, about what happens to those who gaze at the face of the Gorgon – but she still went ahead and looked anyway. If she was determined to find out what I was hiding, she had to take the consequences.

On the other hand, of course – and let's be sensible about this – the responsibility is all mine.

19

The dinner party.

In a short while, I'll tell you what happened before the meal – and what happened after – because they're both part of the same story. But first it's time for you to meet my friends, listen to what they had to say, and find out what we ate.

John arrived first, looking cheerful, which I needed. He was about an hour early, and he'd brought the trotters in jelly and pork scratchings with him. He started unpacking them as soon as he got in the kitchen – from a grubby plastic bag. 'I couldn't find anything else,' he explained. 'Darren keeps nicking the clean ones. I think he goes out after dark and suffocates people.' I put the food in the fridge, on the same shelf as the plate of sausages, and then we started chatting. I told him what I'd done so far, and he told me about work, and so it went on. And he helped me carve the last of the vegetables for the main course: boiled potatoes shaped into pigs, carrots carved into snakes, tomatoes disguised as bald heads, leeks concealed as . . . well, leeks. Some vegetables don't *want* to surrender their soul to creativity.

'What've you got lined up?' John asked, when we'd finished the vegetables (they still needed parboiling, but it could wait until everyone had arrived). So I told him. And if I'd carried a menu card with me, it would have read something like this:

CHEZ FLY

Tonight's Menu

breakfast sausages
boneless pigs' feet in jelly
pork scratchings

consommé

stuffed boar's head
(*with a unique selection of vegetables*)

iced watermelon head

He appeared happy with the choice, which pleased me. There's a little rivalry between us when it comes to food, but nothing serious.

'Is Kate coming later on?' he asked.

I shook my head. 'She can't make it.'

'How come?'

'Stomach. Couldn't face all this rich food.'

'Nothing else?'

'Such as?'

He shrugged. 'I get the impression she doesn't really like us.'

'Well, who knows . . . ? She sounded ill on the phone, though.'

I liked the bit about the phone. *She hadn't been here, she was at home.* He accepted the explanation. People do.

But this is what I was thinking while we were talking: *I know half of the big picture. I've killed one person already – when will I kill the other? And who will it be? One of the guests, perhaps?* But I couldn't see it happening. You don't invite people round to dinner only to stick a knife in their chest.

It's just not polite.

When everyone else was due to arrive, I suggested to John that we lay out the starters on the coffee table in the living room. He advised that I get changed first. I agreed: my thin, black jumper was soaked and stained, even though I'd already had a bath and put on fresh clothes after . . . Well, you know what happened. I undressed in the bedroom, drying myself down and using bandages, plasters and creams as best I could to stop the flow. When I was satisfied there'd be no further leaks, I put on a fresh T-shirt (white), my favourite red jumper (just in case), and a fresh pair of black jeans.

Alison arrived first, on her own, and precisely on time – it was as if she'd been waiting outside the front door counting the seconds on her diver's watch. John asked her how her car was, and she just grimaced and said, 'Very *dry*, John. How's business?' I thought she was being a little over-sensitive . . . Allan, Sue and Nigel all came in Allan's car, at about eight-fifteen, armed with bottles of wine. They were laughing as they came through the door, though I've never found out why, and I guess I never will. Anyway, I shepherded everyone into the living room. Alison had already grabbed the armchair, so Allan and Sue sat on the sofa, while John and Nigel squatted on the floor. I busied myself with drinks for a while, but finally I sat down next to John.

So: the starters. (Though strictly they fall under the category of *nibbles*. Nibbles. I love that word. Nibbles . . .) Everyone tried the pigs' feet first, because they were the most unusual. No one, apart from John and I, managed anything more than faint enthusiasm for them, though there was plenty of laughter, and prodding, and nibbling, and pulling faces, and conversation – so even though four of the trotters were barely touched, they fulfilled some kind of role. The scratchings, on the other hand, were immensely popular, disappearing in seconds. Darren, our apprentice, was responsible for them. (It probably wouldn't please him, even so. *Nothing* pleases Darren. I sometimes wonder if he's had the time and date of his own death revealed to him by an old witch.) The sausages – disappointingly after all my efforts – caused barely a stir, though there were compliments about the unusual flavour. And Alison wanted to know why there were only five.

'I didn't have enough meat,' I told her. 'Doesn't matter, though. I won't eat one.'

'That's OK,' Allan said. 'I don't want mine anyway.' Allan's sentences, almost without exception, rise slowly to fever pitch then fall forcefully to the point, like the arc of an axe blow, or the dive of a bird of prey. It makes him sound ironic even when he doesn't mean to.

'And why *not*, Big Al?' I said, feigning anger (it embarrassed him nonetheless).

'Because I know what goes in them.'

'But these are homemade. You can trust me.'

'Can I?'

'Look, just try one. That's all I ask.'

Five pairs of eyes turned on him, and four voices increased the pressure with positive comments: *Sweet. Succulent. A delicacy. Not to be missed.* And, finally, he caved in:

'Oh, all right then. I'll just have a bite.'

He raised the one remaining sausage to his mouth, and that was the last we saw of it.

'So what *did* you put in them?' Alison asked.

She was getting on my nerves. She hates quiet people, which means that she hates Sue, and me, and Nigel, and Allan. She likes Kate, who was never quiet, and she likes John, to the point where at parties they deliberately arrive separately to convince us there's nothing between them. I often think she only puts up with us for his sake . . . Anyway, Nigel answered her first:

'Old men's willies,' he said. He didn't normally make much of a contribution, and his comic timing was poor, so the shock, more than the humour, made us laugh.

I waited until Allan had finished swallowing before giving her *my* response. 'Rabbit,' I said. 'Lots of herbs and spices, too. But mostly rabbit.'

'You'll have to give me the recipe,' she said, sardonically. Then: 'Where's Kate? Wasn't she supposed to be here?'

John saw that I was getting annoyed, and answered for me: 'She's ill. Some kind of stomach bug.'

'Uh-huh,' she replied. 'It's funny – she didn't mention anything to *me*.' She gave John a look which I'd previously seen on a peacock, and which implied that Kate and I had had an argument. 'Still, there's a lot of it *about*,' she added sarcastically. (I sometimes wonder if Alison gorges herself on sarcasm before she ventures outside, so that she can regurgitate it at innocent passers-by. She's got a huge store of it, and I'm pretty sure she collects any spare she finds lying around, too. John once suggested to me that she rents the flat below and keeps it there, and I believe him.) Anyway, her withering commentary often has the effect of bringing my skin out in a rash, and tonight was a case in point. Everything was made worse by what I'd done to myself this afternoon as well, so that I began writhing on my chair, and had to escape to the kitchen before anyone noticed.

I turned up the heat on the soup and let it simmer, while I laid out the mats, glasses, candles, knives, forks and spoons on the living room table – John lit the candles. After that, I took the boar's head from the oven to do the glazing, then returned it on a low heat; and by the time I'd finished, the consommé was bubbling. A delicious salty, meaty smell. Fine threads of veal in it, and beef. Leeks, celery, carrots. It had been simmering for six hours, and when I served it everyone declared it *a triumph*. Not the usual cry of triumph, which is generally awarded to anything that hasn't been burnt to a crisp, or isn't covered in dog hairs, or doesn't give you bad stomach cramps at three o'clock the next morning, but a genuine *triumph*. I was proud of that soup. If it takes a small mind to be proud of a humble consommé, then mine is the tiniest of all . . . Besides, Alison burnt her hand trying to grab hold of the pan as I served her, which made the experience doubly enjoyable.

I should mention here that there was one moment of concern during the soup course. When it was almost over, and we were all chatting quite comfortably, I began to feel weak and a little sick. Then my chest and legs started to itch, and I felt myself leaking again, and I had to excuse myself and nip off to the bedroom. A few dollops of cream soon sorted it out; but when I replaced the bandages I reinforced them with parcel tape. Nothing sticks like parcel tape. Anyway, when I returned, I observed some dull red stains on my T-shirt. Like a Rorschach test, or some nutty abstract art.

No one noticed.

We moved on to the main course.

It received mixed reactions. The vegetable animals were condemned as *naff* by you-know-who (though no one else laughed *quite* as loudly as she did); however, the boar's head itself was universally well received, with the stuffing and the juices winning the highest praise. The head was a memorable sight. It sat on the table and steamed for quarter of an hour after it was served, its black eyes ignoring us, its snout fixed in a leer. And it's bizarre to see your friends scooping out the inside of an animal's head. It's like witnessing a primitive ritual. Or watching vultures around a carcass.

This is what we talked about while we ate: olives, sausages, pets, the plane crash in the Andes (which I told you about earlier), astronomy, cars, what we remembered from childhood (I told them a little about David), imaginary friends, mirrors, luck, children, and death. The last of these – the conversation about death – was played like a game. I asked the question, *What do you think would be the worst way to die?* and these were the answers:

ALISON: Viciously. Being torn apart by wild dogs. Being shot through the head and dying in incredible pain, very slowly. Being hit by a train and left to lie there, with both your legs broken, and collapsed lungs.

JOHN: I wouldn't like to be cooked alive.

NIGEL: Falling off a cliff. I can't stand heights.

ALLAN: I'd hate to be the Grim Reaper. He'd have to kill himself. He could be having a really good time, scuba diving, or dancing, or talking to someone he really likes, then he'd suddenly get this urge, and his scythe would start quivering, and he'd have to stab himself, and make sure he did the job right first time. It could be very nasty. And while he was doing it he'd be worrying about the administration side. How could he fill in his own death certificate, what if he botched it up? – and so on. That'd be the worst.

SUE: I don't like to think about it.

As for myself, I just made several off-the-cuff suggestions about being caught in a runaway lift, or in a burning building, or drowning, or suffocating. I had a lot of ideas, but the truth is I don't think overmuch about death.

Somewhere in all this someone asked Alison why she kept that shotgun and all those cartridges in her car boot, and she replied, enigmatically:

'Just in case.'

So I said, 'What do you mean?'

And she half-ignored me, which is a great skill, and said, 'There are a lot of crazy people about. More than you'd think . . . Do you know that every morning, from my bedroom window, I could pick off about thirty people going to work?'

We changed the subject.

By the time the boar's head had been thoroughly scooped out, and the vegetables had gone to their own private vegetable hell, we were all relaxed. It's always the way with these evenings of ours. They begin with mutual suspicion, or grudging reticence at best: no one has much to say, and the things that *are* said are brief, or meaningless, or bitter. Everyone thinks to themselves, *I don't know these people. I've got nothing in common with them. My interests are not their interests. Why don't they all just go away and leave me alone?* But then the food gets served, and the haze and heavy air of drunkenness lubricates the charm machine, and the conversations improve. Remarks raise a smile. The background music mellows. There's laughter, and everything is worthwhile again. We all wonder why we've left it so long since we last saw each other. We give out invitations to future events as if we were lovers. And, by the end of the evening, we're all great friends again, prepared, if not to die for each other, then at least to suffer a bad knee or a sore thumb for a few days . . . The fact that the next morning brings with it feelings of shame, and embarrassment, and unabashed scrutiny of everyone else's faults, and an overwhelming urge to cry off all the invitations, is unimportant. The moment is all.

At the end of one such moment, John stood up and wandered towards the hallway. I guessed correctly that he was heading for the toilet, and he was quite surprised when I asked him not to. I told him that there had been some flooding, and that something had broken inside the cistern – but he waved away my explanation.

'I'll just have to nip outside then,' he said cheerily. 'Anyone else want to come?' He was drunk. Not enough to make him fall over, but enough to make this invitation seem normal. Alison was the only one who took him up on it, though whether she needed to was another matter. Nigel then suggested he'd come if he could hold John's dick, and after that things started getting silly – so I stood up, led them quickly through to the kitchen and unlocked the back door.

John disappeared into the darkness. In a horror film he'd never be seen again, but I distinctly saw him grubbing around in the long grass (I *never* mow the lawn) searching for a suitable spot to relieve himself. Alison, slightly unstable after four glasses of wine, was following her nose around the kitchen, making remarks about the washing up, the sausage machine, and all the effort I'd put in. Then the shortbread tin caught her eye.

'Shortbread,' she said. 'I *love* it. Is there any left?'

I shook my head and said no, thinking that would be enough.

It wasn't, of course. She reached up for the tin, clawed it free from the shelf, and dropped it onto the fridge. She apologized, grinning – then she tried to pull off the Sellotape seal. I heard the Skin rattling around inside, and so did she. 'Well, there's *something* in here,' she said, shaking the tin. 'And it's *heavy*. A nice, moist, juicy piece of shortbread . . . Can I have it?'

'If there *is* anything in there, it's not shortbread,' I said, throwing her a look which suggested she should mind her own business. It missed her by a mile. 'But whatever it is – and I don't like to *think* what it could be – it's probably rancid. I've had that tin for years.'

She waved her finger at me in mock admonition. 'You've got a nasty little secret, haven't you?'

I rolled my eyes, and grabbed the tin, and she was too drunk to pursue the argument – though she managed to add a few scathing comments about how battered the tin was, and how it smelled funny, and why was there a Scalpel on the shelf next to it, and where had John gone? But eventually, meeting no resistance, she wandered out of the door like a stray sheep, looking for something to nibble at and shouting forlornly for

John. And my rash, which had flared up again while I was talking to her, left as soon as she did.

I must be allergic to her voice.

Back in the living room, Sue, Allan and Nigel had migrated from the dining area to the coffee table, and when I came in they were discussing suicide. That's what happens when you leave three depressives alone in a room for five minutes. I sat down and listened.

'I don't know how I'd do it,' said Nigel. 'I don't know whether I *could*.'

'I think the best way,' Allan said, 'is to plug your ears, put on a blindfold and get someone to tie you to a railway track.'

'You'd still feel the vibrations when the train approached, though.'

'And it wouldn't be suicide if someone helped you,' Susan added.

'It was just a suggestion,' Allan muttered.

I joined in at this point, contributing a few brief comments – I can be brief when necessary – about how David and I would lie in the road at night waiting for cars; and how I used to dare myself to climb onto factory roofs and stand at the edge, looking down. And Nigel said:

'Didn't you ever get the urge to just let go, and fly, and fall?'

And I was about to tell him I never did, but Sue interrupted:

'I've had that . . . I've often felt that way.'

And then Allan said something about how death was only palatable if you took control of it yourself, and Sue said she'd thought seriously about suicide in the past, and then things started getting *really* depressing. I'll spare you the details. But it's a general rule that whenever four quiet, introspective, miserable people are gathered together, the conversation switches to philosophical speculation on death or terminal shyness, someone threatens to cry, and everyone has a suicide story to tell. Fortunately, after about ten minutes John and Alison returned with beaming faces, and saved us all from mutually assured destruction.

While we're on the subject of misery, I met Nigel in the market last Monday. Neither of us wanted to meet, we tried to avoid bumping into each other, but it couldn't be helped. And then we didn't have much to say anyway, and – well, here's the conversation, so you can see for yourself:

NIGEL: Hello.

ME (trying to sound enthusiastic): Hi, Nige.

NIGEL: How's things?

ME: Things is all right with me. How's things with you?

NIGEL (obviously getting bored already): All right, I suppose.

ME (feigning interest): Where are you off to?

NIGEL (feigning enthusiasm): Oh. Just *about*. You know.

ME (trying to inject some humour): About? Sounds like an interesting place to go.

NIGEL (looking at his watch): It isn't.

ME (annoyed that he looked at his watch, when I was trying to make it obvious that I was as bored with him as he was with me): Well . . . S'pose I'd best be off, then.

NIGEL: Yeah . . . See you later, crocodile.

ME: In a while, alligator.

This last exchange was a routine it's taken us eight months to create, and pretty much represents the height of my conversational skills. But don't get me wrong. I like Nigel, and I think he likes me. It's just this bumping-into-people-in-the-street business. It gets you down.

'What's for dessert?' John asked.

'Alcohol,' Allan suggested.

I cleared the dining table – refusing the usual half-hearted offers of assistance – and dumped the washing up in the kitchen sink. Then I rustled up half a dozen dessert dishes and went to the freezer for the iced watermelon head. I had to avoid the other things, of course, and I checked to see that no one was sneaking up on me while the lid was open . . . Anyway, of all the courses I prepared tonight, the watermelon is the one of which I'm proudest, so forgive me if I take a moment to describe it.

Imagine a watermelon. Imagine holes carved in it, creating a face like the pumpkin heads on Halloween. Imagine the scooped-out watermelon chunks chopped up and mixed with icing sugar and lemon juice, and frozen to create a blood-red, frosted filling. Imagine the head packed with this filling, and the top replaced, so that it looks as if some kind of bloody gunge is bursting out of the eyes and mouth and nose. You've just imagined what I served to my guests.

I double-checked that the freezer was firmly closed before returning to the living room. Everyone was laughing at Sue, who was using her rubber band trick to imitate a monkey. I served the head without fuss or ceremony, and received universal praise, though I was a bit resentful that I didn't have to play down a round of applause, as you sometimes see happening in films.

'What's the filling?' asked Alison.

'The boar's brains,' I lied. A bad joke: everyone gave me queer looks. 'No. I'm only kidding. It's actually the heart.' A worse joke: I was digging my own grave. 'Watermelon and icing sugar, and a bit of lemon juice,' I said quickly – then added, in the manner of a circus ringmaster, 'Eat, eat, *eat!*'

And so they did.

Though for some reason Sue kept the rubber bands on.

'Coffee?' I asked, later.

The table looked like the aftermath of a massacre. Red stains everywhere. A scooped-out head. A bent spoon (Allan had been too vigorous in his appreciation). And six anthropoids, like the things they'd eaten, stuffed with dinner. I offered them chocolate digestives with the coffee, but no one was interested. This was fortunate, considering that I needed the Biscuits later on.

The mention of coffee sparked the departure. I couldn't have done a better job of getting rid of them if I'd turned on all the taps, played a video of a waterfall, and steered the conversation towards toilets, urine and going home quickly. If the bathroom had been available they'd have stayed longer, and I probably wouldn't be here now. (But then, I wouldn't be here now if I hadn't had to pretend that the toilet was broken in the first place. It's a circular argument.)

These are the excuses they gave for leaving:

ALISON: Well, I *must* be off. It's been a lovely evening, and a wonderful meal, and thank you.

ALLAN: I'm knackered.

NIGEL: Bye. (No reason given.)

SUE: I've got a party tomorrow morning, and if I don't get some sleep I'll end up swearing and spitting at the kids.

After everyone else had gone, John helped me clear the table. We talked about Alison, and whether there was anything between them, but he denied it. He said that *he* thought that *she* thought that *he* fancied *her*, but that he *didn't*, or that he *thought* he didn't, but you could never be sure unless you *really* thought about it, which he hadn't much, and even then not. I told him he was talking gibberish, and he became very guarded and refused to hear a bad word spoken against her until he left. Oh – and as he was going, he said,

'I'll call you tomorrow.'

He staggered through the door, and I closed it firmly behind him. It was only eleven o'clock.

What could be more normal than that?

20

This is what happened *before* the dinner party:

After the accident, I—

No, erase that. After I'd *killed* her I sat down by her body and cried. I don't know how long it was, but something strange happened in the meantime. The body, her body, lying there next to me – it wasn't Kate any more. It had no specific identity. It was thirteen million inactive nerve cells, five million hairs, sixty thousand miles of arteries, two hundred bones, fifteen square feet of skin, ten gallons of water. Enough iron for a one-inch nail. Enough fat for seven bars of soap. Enough phosphorous for two thousand matches. Six hundred and fifty limp muscles, one hundred useless joints, eight pints of clotting blood.

But it wasn't *her*.

*　　*　　*

OK. Let's get some facts clear from the start. First, I meant this to be a happier story than it's turned out; but the events control you, not the other way round. *Everything*, as my father once said, *is like it is*. Second, from what I've told you so far, you might be thinking that I ate my girlfriend.

Not true.

Or you might think that if I *didn't* eat her, I served her up for my guests as stuffing for the boar's head, or as that certain *je ne sais quoi* in the consommé, or as colouring and texture for the iced watermelon.

Not true.

You might think, then, that something unusual happened to Kate's body, and it's connected with the dinner party in some way, and eating plays a part, and there's a Rite of Cutting involved somewhere, and the Fifth Object has something to do with it all.

True. But not the whole truth.

Here's what happened.

The first thing I did was empty out the contents of Kate's bag and rearrange all her personal stuff on the bathroom shelf. In the back of my mind I had this vague idea of creating some kind of shrine. Obviously, I've had to abandon it: a shrine without worshippers is meaningless. It's like a hollow egg. Next, I picked up the joke Lighter and positioned it on the lowest shelf – where it is now – and then, I'm ashamed to say, I threw up. Fortunately, I reached the toilet bowl in time. Anyway, after flushing this embarrassment away, I dragged the body slowly into the kitchen. It was very heavy, and it left a red trail, most of which I was able to clean up later, except for a black patch on the carpet in the hallway, which no one seemed to notice. I laid it out on the kitchen floor and returned to the bathroom, where I collected the knife and David's burnt Skin. I returned the Skin to the shortbread tin, sealing it with Sellotape.

What happened next is a little hazy: the precise details have been lost in the general fog. I remember crying again, though I can't remember why, and I remember removing all the clothes from the body and examining every inch of skin: stroking it, breathing in the purity, feeling the fine hair beneath my fingertips. (It was an act of reverence, of worship – but it *wasn't* sexual. That would have been perverse, and disloyal to Kate.) And after it all, I had to decide what to do with the corpse. I couldn't bury it: it would take too long, and I had to prepare dinner. Besides, it was daylight, and there was every chance of being seen by the neighbours (people should mind their own business, but they don't). I could have left it in the garage and locked the door, but I didn't know how long it would have to remain there, and after a while it would start to smell. A couple of other ideas suggested themselves too, but none seemed suitable . . . So that's how the body ended up in the freezer in the hall. I reckoned I could keep it there as long as I needed to, until the right time came; and it wouldn't decompose, and – well, there were all sorts of advantages.

But there was one big problem, too: it wouldn't fit.

To cut a long story short, I did a spot of carving. I won't bother you with the details. I had the equipment from the shop – a clean saw, a carving knife and a cleaver – and once I'd put aside my initial reservations, it was relatively easy work. You have to detach yourself, or the job will never get done. There was only one major sawing task, which took considerable time and effort because the skin and bone in that area were very tough. But it was all over within half an hour.

And then I had the Big Idea. It had been gnawing at the back of my head for some time, and I couldn't kill it, so I had to set it free. I looked at the body, and at the Sausage Filler, and a unique, new ritual suggested itself. If I was to deconstruct the logic of that moment, the links would look something like this:

1. The body has five fingers on its right hand.
2. Those fingers held the Lighter that burnt David's Skin.
3. An act of such violence demands retribution.
4. Retribution must fit the crime.
5. The fingers must be exchanged for the Skin that was destroyed.

So I took the carving knife, and the cleaver, and executed a quick chop followed by a long, precise incision up the length of the forefinger on the right hand. I won't describe the noise, or what it looked like, because neither are very pleasant. All I *will* say is that there's a lot more to a hand than you'd imagine. All sorts of stringy veins, and muscle fibres, and joints, and fat. If you were in the right frame of mind, you might regard the whole thing as art; but I found it deeply disturbing. Separating the flesh from all the other bits was the most fiddly part – it was such a *mess*. If the logic of the ritual hadn't demanded it, I don't think I could have coped.

The hairs were the next problem, but the solution wasn't too far away. I unlocked the door to the garage, filled the scalding tank with a little water – just enough for the meat to be covered – and flicked the switch. When the temperature gauge showed a hundred and forty-seven degrees, and the water was bubbling, I collected the five pieces of finger skin from the kitchen, fixed them to a skewer and lowered them into the water, turning when necessary. After a few minutes the flesh was tender enough to remove some of the hairs by hand. The rest I scraped off with the carving knife.

After that, I left the skin in the fridge to cool down.

It was time to clean up. My arms were covered in blood up to the elbows, with thick black hairs sprouting through. (I realized abruptly, and with some pleasure, that this image corresponded to one of the thought-pictures I'd experienced as a child.) After sponging off and mopping up some of the blood, I wrapped the body in several large freezer bags and a couple of refuse sacks, and carried everything to the freezer. My arms were shivering with the cold as I tried to fit everything in . . . And I couldn't quite manage it. There's a lot of frozen meat in there already, and it would have been stupid to let it spoil, so I had to leave out the biggest piece: the thing now standing in the sink. There were a few other odds and ends, too. I threw away what was left of the right hand, apart from the bones – which, as a final act in the ritual, I cast into the toilet bowl. (They were bright red this afternoon, but the last time I looked, just before I was sick again, they were clean and white.)

Am I boring you?

I hope not. I need to get these details out.

So what next? I had to interrupt the cleaning because of the consommé. This was about two-thirty. It only took about ten minutes to get all the ingredients together and scrape them into the pan, but it gave me some relief from the day's events. With the soup simmering, I switched on the water for a bath. It was still quite warm from this morning, but I prefer to be *boiled*. While I was waiting, I mopped up all the remaining blood outside the bathroom, cleaned off the carving knife, cleaver and saw, emptied the scalding tank, checked that all the food that needed to be ready *was* ready, and then ran the bath. I spread towels on the floor to cover the red stains and other bits and pieces in the bathroom, and lay there slowly cooking for a good half hour – it was the only time I've felt relaxed all day. Of course, there was a lot of blood in the bath – I was still quite pink when I emerged – but the experience *soothed* me, and gave me fresh impetus to continue with the food. I couldn't see it then, but I can now: the preparations for dinner helped me avoid facing up to what I'd done.

After drying myself off I prepared the iced watermelon – slicing, adding the icing sugar, and then the preliminary freezing. I also scrubbed and stuffed the boar's head, and bunged it in the oven. This takes plenty of patience and skill – something people just don't have the taste for these days. For example, in the first place, you've got to get hold of a well-shaped head with short ears; then you've got to bone it (making sure you leave the snout bone in); then you need to sew up the mouth; and finally you've got to stick it in brine for four days. That's the hard bit. The fun comes when you stuff it with sausage meat, cubed pork tongues, hard boiled eggs, pistachio kernels and bacon – until the whole thing looks as if it's about to burst.

The last bit of preparation involved the sausages – I now had my own special filling, of course – and when I'm making them at home I always consult the Fifth Object: my Butcher's Manual. This is my favourite Object, and by far the most useful. Not a day goes by when I don't scour it for something or other, and today I needed the recipe for Breakfast Sausages: salt, pepper, back fat, water, cornflour, sausage binding, mace, ginger, lean pork, and that extra special ingredient, the speciality of the house, *viande de doigt*. Finger flesh, to you. It didn't take long – I had all the ingredients ready and my Butcher Boy Electric Sausage Filler to hand – but there was only enough meat for five. I cooked them in the oven for about an hour, then fried them in a little oil, and put them in the fridge to cool off.

While they were in the oven, I performed the first of to-day's three Rites of Cutting (the third one – the pentagon of sausages – you already know about). I found the Scalpel – I keep it by the book of dreams, underneath the mattress in the bedroom. Without a blade attached, obviously; otherwise all that groping about trying to find it would end in a few sliced fingers. The fresh blades are stored separately, in their own foil wrapper.

So: I found the Scalpel, slid a blade onto it, then stripped off all my clothes and returned to the kitchen. I gathered some bandages and plasters from the medicine cabinet, and a needle and thread from the sewing basket in the living room, and carried everything into the bathroom. I sat down on the edge of the bath, placed everything on the chair, took the Scalpel in my right hand, and began the ritual. I said, *In the moment of their meeting both skin and steel are one*, then I made the first incision on my chest, near the left arm, just below the collar bone. The flesh fell away beneath the blade, and I dug deep, drawing it down past the left nipple, alongside the round of my belly, over the hip bone, down the thigh, and on to the kneecap – one long, deep, crooked line, like the Great Rift Valley in Africa. It caused so much pain, and the blood flowed so easily, running the full length of my body, that it was – I'm struggling for the word – it was *sweet*. I felt giddy, and so happy. And in the end words *can't* explain it: it's something

that can only be known and never described, as John might say
. . . Anyway, the blood went everywhere. On the towels, on
the bath, on the thing in the sink, in the toilet bowl, on the
toilet seat, and the cistern, and the windows, and the walls.
There was no point in trying to clean it up; I didn't have
enough time. It also went all over me, but that's partly my own
fault: I rubbed most of it in with my fingers, on my legs, and
back, and torso, though not on any part of the body that would
be exposed during the dinner party.

I made five cuts in all: one along the length of each arm,
from the shoulder to the wrist; one each on the left and right
side of my chest, running down to the knees; and one right
down the middle of my torso, bisecting the navel and passing
to the base of my penis. Naturally, after each gash, the Rite
demanded that I announce: *It is almost done. I promise to end
what I have begun.* And when I'd finished, when the towels
beneath my feet were soaked in blood and the pain had gone
way beyond pleasure, I was obliged to say: *It is done. Skin and
steel are no longer one, and I have ended what I began. I offer this
blood, this blade and this cut flesh to the past, present and future.*
Sounds simple, doesn't it? The truth is, my hand was shaking
so violently by the time I got to the last Cutting, that particular
wound was more zigzag than line. I think it was my body's way
of telling me to stop. But sometimes you *can't*.

At the end of it all, I tossed the Scalpel onto the floor
and picked up the needle and thread. It's generally a good idea
to sterilize the needle in these circumstances, but it seemed
stupid, given what I'd planned, so I didn't bother. I just
stitched the wounds, one after the other. Big, wide, looping
stitches . . . It was the closest I've come to experiencing agony
in my life – but it had to be done, and I was proud to have
finished it. The antiseptic cream came next; soothing, cooling,

like cold water on a burn. Then the bandages, wrapped tightly around my chest and arms. It took ages to wrap them and pin them together, because I didn't want to move my arms, and each new contact between bandage and wound caused new pain. Even when I'd finished, when I'd used up most of the rolls, there was blood seeping through.

Then what? I washed the blood from my hands, and the few splashes that had spotted my neck and face; and I cleaned the needle, dried myself, pulled the blade from the Scalpel – keeping the thin film of blood intact – and returned to the bedroom, armed with the last remaining bandages. I got dressed, left the Scalpel by the shortbread tin in the kitchen, and checked the food. The sausages were ready, so I removed them from the oven and put them on a plate in the fridge.

I felt a bit down, I must admit. I don't know if it was the pain, or the killing, or the futility of it all. Perhaps I was just exhausted. I didn't bother writing a record, or taking a photograph, or storing any of the blood. There didn't seem to be any point. I decided to keep the Scalpel blade, though; and as I was putting it in the box in the garage, there was a knock at the door.

It was John.

This is what happened *after* the dinner party:

John was the last to leave, and as I closed the door behind him I felt something trickle down my left wrist. Blood, from the shoulder. One of the bandages had worked loose. The stitch was inadequate, too – a big, clumsy, loose bow. A couple of extra stitches on the more obvious wounds and a yard or two of parcel tape did the trick; but it was only a patch job. There was more Cutting to be done.

I went to the bathroom, where I threw up again and relieved my bladder, which had been set to burst all evening. Please don't misunderstand me: retching and urinating over five white finger-bones is not, even under such extraordinary circumstances, something I'm happy with. It seemed offensive at the time, and it feels even more disrespectful now. And I couldn't bear to flush . . . When I'd finished, I switched on the water for my final bath of the day – which continues to this moment – went into the kitchen, drank a cup of coffee, ate half a dozen glucose tablets to keep me going, and finally made up my mind about what I ought to do. I also found the packet of chocolate Biscuits. Then I went to the living room and grabbed the cassette recorder and three cassettes, and placed them on the chair in the bathroom. The tapes weren't entirely blank: during this recording, I've wiped over my entire collection of Pinky and Perky singles, and Pink Floyd's *Animals*, and *Meat is Murder* by The Smiths, and Nirvana's *In Utero*.

I returned to the kitchen and brought the Sausage Filler, the Scalpel, the Butcher's Manual, and the Skin from the short-bread tin, and placed them by the Lighter on the lowest shelf in the bathroom, in the order I described at the beginning of this narrative. These are the Five Objects which best represent what happened to me today. Then, with a sharp kitchen knife, I carved out a protective circle of Symbols around each Object, the patterns repeated until the chain was complete: the rabbit's foot, the naked flame, the bicycle, the erect penis and the razor-sharp blade. These are the Five Symbols which summarize what happened to me *before* today.

There was still work to be done.

I took the Scalpel and attached a fresh blade to it, ready for today's second Rite of Cutting. I was apprehensive, because of the pain I'd suffered this afternoon – but it was only cowardice. You can't avoid the inevitable.

I positioned myself over the toilet bowl, so that some of the blood from the Cutting would drip into the water and mix with the urine, vomit and bones. Then I started with my penis, repeating the words as before: *I give this blade to my body; I give my body to this blade*, and so on. This was probably the most awkward Cutting I've ever performed. I refused to stimulate myself to an erection, for reasons which I hope you'll understand, so I had to deal with flaccid flesh. It needed firm handling, too. It was like a leech. It kept slithering out of my grasp; and I had to be careful to avoid the central vein. Even so, there was a frightening amount of blood . . . But the *pain*. The pain was *beautiful*. There's no other word . . . The design itself – a leech, of course – was a nice touch, I thought.

Next I turned the blade on my own hands. On the left palm I carved the Lighter, scraping away the flesh at the top, near the base of my middle finger, to create a raw, red flame. On the right palm, with my left hand, I carved the Scalpel itself (a pretty poor effort). On the back of the left hand I cut a fair representation of the mirror in the bathroom, complete with angular crack and wooden frame. On the back of my right hand I attempted a likeness of Kate's head, but it's too small to do it justice, and the image has red hair, which just isn't right, considering how black the real thing is. But nothing's perfect.

Then I made two final carvings.

The first was on the thing in the sink. Simple, but appropriate.

The second was on my own face. By this time I'd run out of suitable ideas: I couldn't do another blade or another face, so I opted for the free, creative, inspirational approach. More importantly, I decided to wreak revenge on the mirror man. (If you ever find yourself in this situation, remember that you have *ultimate control*. Whatever you do, your alter ego on the other side of the glass is obliged to copy you.) So I held the Scalpel in my right hand, and uttered the appropriate words, and made the appropriate observances – and I drew the blade down each cheek five times, from the eyes to the chin. As if I was crying blood. But this wasn't enough – it never is – so I cut horizontal parallel lines from the left ear to the right, ten in all, creating a surreal, but not displeasing, checkerboard effect. (It was excruciatingly painful, of course; but pain is irrelevant.)

Then I laughed. I could see the anguish and disappointment on the mirror man's scarred face. He looked so *depressed*.

Well, there was a lot of blood, but I had the needle and thread ready. I didn't need them for the cuts on my face, or hands, or penis, because these wounds were relatively light, and formed a crust after a few minutes anyway; but I was about to have a bath, so I needed to tighten up the earlier wounds. I removed the bandages, then hooked stitches in the gaps where the threads were most widely spread. Arms, legs and torso, tight as a drum. No leaks. Like the boar's head must have felt, stuffed full of flesh and blood, sewn up at the back like a straitjacket. When I'd stopped dripping and dribbling, I picked up all the towels and threw them into the hallway. I had no need for them, nor any need to hide them. There was still blood on the floor, and in the sink, but it didn't bother me . . . Then I ran the water into the bath, examining myself as it filled. Stitches like little black spiders on the skin. Red weals like lipstick marks. Rough wound ridges. Mannequin flesh.

I put the cassette in the recorder and stepped into the bath when it was almost full. It was hot – scalding – but I immersed myself all the same. So much pleasure. The streaked red wounds and the warmth reminded me of my time in the womb, and the red wet stains recalled my own birth. So I pressed RECORD on the cassette player, and said: *Let's be honest.*

The rest you know about.

Here are some thoughts I'd like to offer as a general summary, before I switch off . . . Bear with me. It won't take long.

1. I can't think of a single word that adequately describes what's happened to me today – though the one that immediately springs to mind is *excessive*.
2. If I'd been vegetarian, would things have turned out differently?
3. You have a choice. I didn't discover this until it was too late. You definitely have a choice. (I hope I don't need to explain.)
4. Here's my final thought-picture. It clearly shows this bath, filled with blood, and a bloated white body floating in it. Although it doesn't directly suggest that I cut my throat in five places, I can read between the lines. My Decision is simple: the second killing must be my own.
5. I think I might have left the gas on.

OK. *It is almost done. I promise to end what I have begun.* I'm switching off the recorder now. Wait for it . . . Switching off—

Hold on, though. I still haven't told you what I've got wedged in the sink, swimming in all that blood. How *remiss* . . . Those of you who've already guessed what it is can stop listening right now, and get on with the gardening, or whatever it is that keeps you from harm. Those of you who haven't . . . Well, it's Kate's head, of course. It's a small, pretty head with a thick mane of black hair, and it's been looking down at me all night. In that way she had, with her thin lips curled down. Oh – and in the centre of her forehead I've carved a rabbit's foot. A better one, this time; much better than the meaningless scar on my own body.

You might be wondering *why* her head is there. And what can I say? It bothers me, too. But, in the end, there's only one answer I can give—

Why not?